Soon, She Must

HJ FURL

Copyright © 2023 / 2024 by HJ Furl

All rights reserved. No part of this publication may be reproduced or transmitted, in any form or by any means, without permission of the publishers or author. Excepting brief quotes used in reviews.

Any reference to real names and places are purely fictional and are constructs of the author. Any offence the references produce is unintentional and in no way reflects the reality of any locations or people involved.

Creative cover design, book format, and textual enhancement by Hammad at:

www.hmdpublishing.com

'I generally avoid temptation...unless I can't resist it.'
— caption on a fridge magnet.

For everyone who is still trying to lose weight.

fat

She lies on the crumpled bed, slides the needle into the soft flesh of her inner thigh, depresses the plunger, injects the serum and purges herself of her nasty, flabby, excess fat. At least, that's what the peeling label on the phial promises her. If she sticks to her balanced low-calorie diet, exercises regularly and controls her pangs of hedonic hunger. Which she doesn't. Her issue is that she lacks the will to succeed. She gives in too easily.

Purge over for yet another restless night, she calms, her rib cage rising then sinking. She holds a damp swab over her puncture wound and slips the damned prickle out of her, laying it to rest in its cheap, pink, plastic kidney dish. To be disposed of later, with all her other contaminated sharps.

'There, that wasn't so bad, was it?' she says, exhaling, kidding, herself, 'Hardly felt it, did you?' She knows, the purge will always hurt her, 'Still, I suppose, if it helps me shed all my ugly fat?'

She draws back the curtains to see the cruel night. The cul-de-sac is silent for once. There are no fire sirens screaming down Main Street, no building works, home restorations or birds singing, to invade her inner peace. She shuts them out, sits sideways-on, on the edge of her bed in just her worn black hipster pants and inspects her body shape in front of the gilt-edged mirror on the wall.

'See all the sore red weals where your bra and pants cut grooves in your fatty flesh, Vicki?'

Stressed out, she lies on the bed and tries to relax, her legs and arms flopped uselessly on the bed. After weeks of daily injections, she has failed to see any changes in her body. She is still the same fat, pudgy, fed-up girl she was when lockdown deprived her of a blossoming career in fast food pasta retail management running the rundown *Café Amalfitano* in Main Street.

Her odious brother suggested, since she is a stickler for detail with A-levels in English and a deep love of books, she take up proof reading, advertising her services online. Demand for her critically sharp yet fair pair of eyes from busy writers astonished her. She never returned to the café. Instead, with help from her wealthy mother, she took out a mortgage on a hovel in a quiet cul-de-sac off a side street: a single garage converted into a bedroom-bathroom-kitchenette. There she immersed herself, correcting the constant flow of manuscripts that fluttered like the first welcome butterflies of Spring through her brass letterbox.

She made a lot of money. Made herself really fat. At least, that's how she feels she looks. Gross.

She keeps her scales on a square tile of black lino in a corner of the bedroom. Drained, exhausted, she climbs up on the scales, alarmed to discover her BMI has soared high as twenty-seven, which means that she is obese in her distrait mind: five feet six inches tall, thirty-three inches around her waist, weighing in at one hundred and fifty-five pounds.

Ashamed of herself, hiding her body from view, she dresses quickly in a black vest, loose-fitting jeans and anklets. Checks the time: three-thirty: the small hours. The alarm shrieks just as she is making the bed. She switches it off, zips her pink Amalfi 4-wheel, hard shell, medium-sized case then waits for her taunting hunger pangs to return.

Vicki hides her treats on a high-up shelf in the cupboard in the kitchenette. She puts the kettle on, takes down a floral china teacup, dispenses four sweeteners then adds a peppermint tea bag from her glass-topped wooden boxed selection: to help her sleep. Bread she stores in a cream enamelled metal bread bin with a fawn wheatsheaf on the top. She flips the lid and lifts out the wholemeal sourdough loaf she bought in the fashionable new bread shop in town a day ago. It feels hard, firm, crusted, in her grip. It's going stale and needs eating up. She pulls the bread board out of its stand, draws a serrated knife out of its wooden block, sets the loaf, and prepares to slice. One slice or two? She carves herself three tranches of sourdough.

The toaster has three wide slots designed to take crumpets, bagels, doorstops of bread. She slots the chunks into the toaster, eying the shallow glass butter dish by the bread bin. The butter is soft: perfect for spreading. Opening the cupboard, she reaches up and takes down an unopened jar of crunchy peanut butter. The label on the jar says this brand is one hundred percent free of palm oil. It has a strip of red tamper-proof cellophane round the top. She breaks the seal, tears it off, and unscrews the lid, baulking at the layer of fatty oil covering the peanuts.

The kettle boils: she makes tea. Her toast pops up: she smothers it with butter, daubing it in dollops of delicious oily, fatty, crunchy peanut butter. Goes to bed and eats it all. Stomach full, bloated with fatty food, hunger pang satiated, at least for now, she lets the mint tea calm her back to sleep.

Soon, she must try to lose some of her repulsive fat, she really must.

The pale grey twilight fades into daylight streaming through the crack in the curtains to dance on her eyelids. She opens her eyes, rolls on her side, gropes for the alarm clock and checks the time: almost seven. She only managed three hours sleep. Gail said it's imperative that she gets a restful night's sleep, an absolute minimum of eight hours every night if she is to have the strength to lose her body fat.

Her bowel is blocked, heavy, swollen: the constipated effect of eating excessive amounts of fatty stodge in the middle of the night and drinking insufficient fluid. She tumbles out of bed, visits the toilet, strains, and strains. When she wipes herself clean, the tissue is streaked with bright scarlet oxygenated blood. Unable to stem the tears, she flushes the toilet, angrily slamming the cracked oaken lid closed, goes to the kitchenette and drinks a litre of water.

Utterly dejected, she surfs the internet until she finds a brutal crash starvation diet that promises to lose her a stone in weight in ten days.

This is useless, she thinks, I'll last a day then I'll start eating again. I won't shed a single pound.

cure

At last, a ray of light. Inside the glossy pages of Elting and Meerton's hyper-local monthly *Vista* magazine, beneath an advertisement for trusted ready-mix concrete, lurks a small ad for a remedy shop. Better still, the shop appears to specialize in common dietary challenges such as fat cutting elimination, obesity, diabetes, alcoholism, slimming, cholesterol cuts - and a new branch has just opened in Elting.

After a satisfying breakfast of pork sausages, baked beans, streaky bacon, fried bread, fried eggs and orange juice, she gets up, cleans her teeth, showers then dresses in her baggy cream sweatshirt with a strawberry motif, black pull-on cargo trousers, and trainers.

It is spitting sleet outside when she opens the curtains. Wearing her best danger red lightweight puffer jacket, she grabs her key and leaves. The cutting wind nips at her cheeks. The cul-de-sac is deserted. The remedy shop is a healthy fifteen minutes' walk for her. God knows, she could do with the exercise, couldn't she?

The shop reminds her of an olde-fashioned apothecary she visited with her mother when she was a little girl in a quaint picture-box village on the Suffolk coast. The walls are steeped to the ceiling with mahogany glass-fronted cabinets full of brown glass bottles with opaque stoppers, faded buff labels, glass phials, conical flasks, test tubes: a veritable laboratory for concocting cures.

In front of the nearest wall stretches a glass display counter with a single silver bell. The poker-faced shop assistant is slumped against it, her head propped up on her left arm, blunt fingernails scratching a red spot under her ear, wearing a pristine white lab coat unbuttoned at the front to show a dawn blue tee-shirt.

Vicki notices her sleeve is undone: the girl's forearm is pale as goat's milk, lightly freckled, and she has high cheekbones. Her auburn hair is tied back off her face in an attractive tight plait which tumbles out of sight down her back. The girl is disinterested in her. So, she rings the service bell.

'There's no need for that,' the girl barks in a taut accent without adjusting her posture, 'Yes? Can I help you?'

'I feel really tired. My back hurts bad. I sweat hard. I eat too much. I'm fat. I want to lose weight.'

The girl shakes her head, at her, vigorously, 'I do not find you fat. I do not think you need to lose fat. If you ask me, you have a gut figure.'

'You mean good.'

'I meant gut.'

Vicki looks round the empty shop searching for a good excuse, 'I want to look good for the beach.'

The girl's face tans at the mention of the word beach, 'Ah, which beach do you wish to look good for?'

'It's a secret.'

'Ach, I am good at keeping secrets. I promise not to tell no-one. Cross my part and hope to die.'

'Heart,' says Vicki correcting her, annoyed at her appalling grammar, 'I didn't come here to chat. I need a drug to stop me feeling hungry all the time and eating too much. What do you suggest?'

'I am sorry. I am new to this country. No-one ever speaks to me like you are. Is it my accent?'

'If you ask me, I think you have a lovely accent.'

'Thank you for being so kind to me. Have you tried my hand-made stodge?'

Vicki hasn't tried it, 'No, what's stodge?'

'Stodge is thick food rich in carbs that is heavy and filling and stops you feeling hungry. You take it three times a day: soon as you wake in the morning, instead of lunch, und when you go to bed. Would you like me to stir one up for you?'

The girl is wearing her gold-effect name badge: Rahel. It isn't a name Vicki is familiar with. She asks her what it means in English.

'It means Rachel.'

'Rachel, that's a lovely name,' lovely just like you, she thinks, then concentrates, 'Yes, I would.'

Rahel turns her back on her and opens the nearest cabinet. Her beautiful handwoven plait stretches as far as her waist ending in a scruffy bit which resembles the end of a horse's skirt. She takes out some glass bottles, pausing to question herself.

'Now, which is the best for her? Ja, this is best,' then she turns to face her only customer today, smiling proudly, 'I have it here for you. Wait, please.'

Vicki giggles childishly: Rahel is so strict! She wonders how the auburn girl would look dressed in a black leather leotard wielding a whip on her back, letting her mind play its creepy dark games.

Out loud she says, 'It's alright, take your time. I'm not going anywhere. I live near here,' and tells her, her name.

'I like that name, Vicki,' Rahel says, musing to herself as she assembles the bottles on the counter.

She disappears in a narrow recess at the far end of the shop, returning several minutes later dressed in an antiquated smock and white lace cap. A curled strand of auburn hair hangs loosely to one side of her face where she didn't pin it back properly, giving her an austere, harsh, disciplined appearance.

Rahel is carrying a conical flask with a grey stopper, a flat round-bottomed flask, like the one she used for practical chemistry at school, and an indescribable glass apparatus with a teapot spout, a vent and tubes sticking out of the top. Serious, sombre, she pours liquid from the bottles into and out of the flasks, reaching under the counter to take out a large white lidded plastic pot of powder, adds the powder and shakes it into a stodge which she ladles into the pot. Stodge stirred she screws on a scarlet plastic lid then passes the gruel to her only customer wrapped in a brown paper bag.

'There,' she sighs, 'Take six scoops three times a day in place of meals. That is ten pounds. Have a gut holiday.'

Vicki pays by card, thanks Rahel, promises to call in to see her sometime soon then steps out into the sleet. The weather has turned bitterly cold. She zips up her puffer jacket as high as her neck, blinking flittering flakes off her eyelids, rubbing her hands. She feels the cold, the cold makes her feel hungry.

She curses herself, 'Why didn't you put on warmer clothes and gloves, stupid girl?' then she jogs home to keep warm.

As soon as she has dried her hair and changed into a warm lemon sweater and cord joggers, she sprints to the kitchen, unwraps the pot, unscrews the lid, extracts its pink plastic measuring scoop and dispenses six heaps of stodge into a cereal bowl. She raises the first spoon to her lips, opens her mouth wide and slides it inside. The slime tastes disgusting, like rancid fat. Retching, she spits the masticated mess out into the sink, rinses her mouth with strong peppermint mouthwash, then brushes her teeth. The stodge she unceremoniously consigns to a waste sack without bothering to recycle its container.

She reaches for the bar of dark cooking chocolate she keeps hidden from view on the top shelf of her kitchen cupboard for her depressing, sad winter moments.

In her last ditch attempt at losing fat, she joins the local gym and signs up for a half-hour personal fitness session with Keira Marsh, a proven specialist in women's fat reduction who uses intensive exercise regimes as her preferred method for restoring the female's muscles, strength and vitality.

habit

The next day is an extremely mild one for the depths of winter, the communal sports centre is an easy walk from home. So, she opts for her black cotton tummy control secret shaping vest, rubber-stretch knee-length shorts and her soft cotton socks. The plate glass door swings open toward her automatically. Although it isn't raining, she still wipes her feet on the grey polymer commercial mat, out of habit.

Vicki sees two wall-mounted moulded plasma screens on her immediate left. Walks over. Reads one. It tells her to tap the screen before she scans her members key fob using the concealed infra-red light. She does all that, taps gym, taps exit, smiles hard at the receptionist with caramel hair in mouse bunches, who is busy blushing her face and doing her nails, sanitizes her hands with froth foam then presses her fob against an infra-red light at the gym entrance. It refuses to open.

She about-turns to face the receptionist who is wearing a Bee badge, 'I can't get the door to open?'

'That's because you didn't tap the screen hard enough. Here, watch me do it for you,' Bee ceases to apply her blusher and stands, revealing her sensational pink party frock and perfect complexion.

She has never met anyone so immaculately made-up. The girl's face resembles a painted puppet's with smooth velvet skin, charcoal eyebrows painted over radioactive pink eyelids, and prominent false lashes, a tiny beauty mole, diamond ear conches, and a miniscule pearl stud in her left nostril. But it's the lurid, squashed, ripe plum flesh smeared over her fat lips, that impresses her the most.

'Where did you get that lipstick?' she asks her, enthusing, 'It looks so awesome and it's so you?'

Bee dips her hand inside her dress pocket and draws out a thick crimson roll-on, 'Do you really think so? It's swollen gland by penis. Stunning isn't it?' she holds the tube up to her face showing off the red-faced faerie tattoo on her left wrist, 'Mm, suits your pale skin, you should try it maybe.'

Before Vicki can ask why she is dressed as a fairytale princess, she takes her fob, prances across to the check-in in her wobbly red stilettoes, steadies herself, and brings her fist down on the screen.

'Thanks,' she says, receiving the fob back as she approaches the glass gym door, 'Appreciated.'

'Don't mention it. Must go. My baby's at a unicorn party. I'm meant to be her dream fairy tonight. In you go. Have a good thrash. Most of all have fun. Live your life to the full. Before it's too late.'

The gym door clicks and opens. Her confidence renewed, uplifted by Bee's remarkable cosmetic surgery and positive can-do attitude, she ventures inside. Inside, the gym is heaving with sweating young men punishing their muscular physiques with weights in strength zone, cycling themselves into frenzies in cardio or posturing, mostly for her attention, on the grey rubber mats in core.

It comes as no surprise to her when the sad dull boys heads swivel to appreciate her breasts and rear. After all, she *is* the only girl present in the gym. Apart from the fit girl sitting on the grubby black rubber box in stretch zone.

'Ignore them, they'll soon leave you alone,' the girl says, patting her box, 'Hey, I'm Keira. You must be the girl who wants to lose all her fat.'

'Well, are you?' she adds.

'My name's Vicki.'

'Sorry, I meant Vicki.'

'Come and sit with me, then.'

Vicki joins her trainer on the box. Their legs touch. It's the first time she has touched anyone in weeks. Touching the girl's legs feels wonderful. Her body feels lovely and warming close up and she seems open to her feelings.

'Open your heart to me. Tell me how you feel. Go on, be honest with yourself. I want to hear your heart speak.'

'If I'm honest, I feel really tired? My back hurts, bad. I sweat, hard. I'm fat. I want to lose weight?'

'I can change your life,' says the shame-faced ginger-red elfin beauty with a lilting hint of brogue.

Keira's vibrant, healthy, and attractive. Her breasts are round, pale, like over-cooked dumplings, kids tennis balls. Great abs, too, pallid milk-white skin, cleft buttocks, lean, sinewy thighs: a body to die for. Vicki wants her for her dollish figure, her slender athletic limbs, her sleek, rakish torso.

Next day, she breezes into the gym in a cream hoodie, high impact sports bra and skin-tight fitness pants. Keira is busy playing on her rubber box, kicking her legs, clutching a notepad. Before Vicki can speak, she points out a set of biometric weighing scales lying ominously on the fitted flatline dark grey sweat-impervious flooring.

'Hey, let's see how much you weigh, shall we?' she says, encouragingly, as if this isn't an ordeal.

Vicki takes off her hoodie, shoes and anklets and mounts the scales which flash up her red digital reading in kilos. Disturbed by the inflated figures, she asks what her weight is - in imperial pounds.

Keira hesitates before replying, 'Like me to take off two pounds for your clothes?'

'Just tell me how much, can you?'

'One hundred and sixty pounds.'

Her vulnerable self-confidence evaporates with the shock, 'What did you just say? How much?'

'I said: one hundred and sixty pounds. Why, how much did you think you weighed?'

'When I weighed myself, I was only a hundred and fifty-five. Can't have put on five pounds in a week, can I?'

The waif rubs her small, blunt chin, and nods at her, painfully slowly, 'Our scales never lie, Vicki.'

'In that case, I need to lose a stone in three months.'

'If you really want to lose that much weight there are changes you must make, like drinking three litres of water every day, working out three times a week, and keeping a daily food diary focusing on your total calorie intake, fat to calorie mix and protein to calorie ratio,' advises Keira, expertly.

Vicki laces her shoes, tying them in double knots. Seems everything comes in threes with Keira. She asks if she can start at two litres of water, work her way up. Three litres *does* seem a lot. Keira listens to her intently, taking notes. The girl has this uncanny aura about her that instils confidence. In her heart, she feels she can lose all her fat, sees a shining light of hope at the end of her bleak tunnel of constant bellyache.

Motivated at last, she asks, 'What does total calorie intake mean? What are fat and protein ratios?'

Keira tells her all will be revealed in a special email. If she'd like to put on her shoes and socks and follow her? For the next half hour, she is put on the treadmill, waggles battle ropes, works a twenty-kilo chess press, is taught how to leg curl, safely, at fifteen-kilos. Keira has her perform sit ups. Forces her to mountain climb the box. Once Vicki is exhausted, they lie flat on their rubber mats intimately close to one another like lovers and stretch. She turns her head to face the girl and delivers her shocking sting in the tail: 'I must achieve my fat loss in three months. If I fail, I'll complain to the management about your service.'

Keira stares at her in disbelief, inhaling deeply, squealing, 'Is this meant to be some kind of joke?'

She studies her bare feet ashamed of herself for what she just said, struggling to climb off the mat.

'I'd rather you didn't make sick jokes, threatening me like that,' the girl chides, acid in her voice.

Vicki pulls on her socks, shoes, and gets up off of the mat, 'I wouldn't dream of threatening you.'

She sanitizes her hands and promptly leaves stretch zone. Mind-in-a-muddle, she presses the red exit button and walks out the door. The brat managed to put on a brave smile but didn't hide her upset. Vicki tries to shake her smarting face off of her mind. She's fallen madly in love with Keira already, if truth be told, and just can't wait to see her again.

energy

The so-called special email hits her inbox next day but, unlike Keira's eyes, there are few aspects of the note Vicki considers special. The first attachment consists of an illegible handwritten scrawl that looks as if it was captured by phone: she can't read it. The second part is an inky, fuzzy, grey, mishmash of hieroglyphics, spider webs, stick insects contorted into shapes and postures she can't discern.

She considers her position with Keira carefully: twenty-five pounds spent, no yield. Yield will be vital to her if her efforts are to lead to successful fat reduction, and Amalfi, in three months' time.

She stops procrastinating over her fitness trainer and concentrates, instead, on her fat consultant. Fat, Gail said, is a lipid vital for her health. Fat gives her energy. It cushions her organs and keeps her body warm. Fat helps her to grow and reproduce. Her excess fat is deposited inside her body.

Too much excess fat could be bad for her.

Angrily, she slides the tip of the needle into her fleshy mass of abdomen, depresses the plunger, and pulls it out, throwing the spent syringe at the ruptured wastepaper basket in the corner of the room, missing - then she calls Gail.

'Weighed myself today,' she says brusquely, 'Put on five pounds in a week. Is that even possible?'

Gail will reply whenever it suits her. Vicki uses her as her placebo: a medical procedure prescribed for her psychological benefit rather than any physiological effect. Despite her strict consultant's subliminal influence and abstract motivational techniques, she feels less confident than ever that she'll achieve her fat goals.

Frustrated, she fires off a blunt email to Keira requesting an urgent review of her fitness training, workouts and overall diet plan - adding that she can't read a thing:

This isn't a reflection on your ability as my trainer. Isn't intended as criticism, she lies, I never felt this hungry for success in my life. Vicki.

The reply hits her tablet seconds later:

Hey, sweetheart, I was only trying to help. Keen to get you started. Achieve those smart goals of yours! How about we meet two weeks' time, Valentine's Day, 930 after gym closes? I'm free if you are.

See you in the gym, then,

Keira.

Sweetheart.

Keira called her sweetheart.

calorie

Mauve and orange crocuses rear their heads above the grassy parapet off the high street. Feeling more upbeat, Vicki sits up in her bed and makes a to-do-list:

Send Keira excel spreadsheet that calculates protein, fat, carb and saturated fat ratios expressed as a percentage of her total calorie intake.

Confirm their review meeting.

Post essential pre-publicity on sports centre's Facebook page.

Book light liquid supper for two.

As soon as she has finished creating the spreadsheet, she emails it to Keira with a covering note:

Hi Keira, can't wait for our review. I've cobbled together my daily fat plan. Thought you'd like to see it before we meet. Weighed myself this morning. I lost four pounds! Four pounds! Think this calls for a celebration, don't you? Are you free to join me for a Valentine's Day Supper at Eva's?

She's thinking cheese sharing platter for two, baked halloumi fingers, humus, pitta, olives, a glass of Malbec for her, glass of Sancerre for Keira, to start with. Famished, having hardly eaten a thing all day, she presses SEND, switches to phone then dials the communal sports centre. She is greeted by an automated ansaphone speaking with a ripe, warming, healthy, plum-in-mouth voice:

'Welcome to Fit-not-Fat. For more information about us, including our opening times, please visit our website at www.fit-not-fat.com. Otherwise, please select one of the following five options. For sales and membership enquiries press 1. For the gym press 2. If your enquiry is about personal training press 3. For adult and kid's party bookings press 4. Alternatively, for all other enquiries, please press 5.'

She presses 5.

She is transferred to a terse woman who answers abruptly with, 'Fit-not-Fat, can I help you?'

'I booked a review for half an hour at nine-thirty, Tuesday, the fourteenth with Keira Marsh. I'd like to pay twenty-five pounds by card,' she says it all in one breath, worried at her breathlessness.

'Can I take your name, please?'

'Hart, Ms Vicki Hart.'

The phone mutes as the woman searches for her personal details, 'Found you. Unusual first name.'

Vicki rolls her eyes round in mild annoyance, 'Really? It's common enough in England, isn't it?'

'Oh, right, yes, of course it is, thanks for that,' the dense woman is muttering daftly in the distance.

She shuts her eyes and imagines Keira lying naked, pallid in the half-light, half her face obscured by clouds, half her face illuminated. Her flames of red hair lit by the sun. Snub nose. Pursed lips. Elfin ears. Her luminescent white skin glowing incandescently. Her adorable, dreamy-teary, eyes.

Unusual girl, her china doll.

'If I can take the long number on your card when you're ready? Hello, Ms Hart. Are you there?'

Unusual girl, like her.

Vic pays for her session, cuts the call then visits Fit-not-Fat's Facebook page to post her feedback:

Thank you from the bottom of my heart for changing my life, Keira. You're a credit to fitness, an inspiration to me in my quest to achieve my fat loss goals, and a lovely, wonderful human being.

Publicity leaked, she opens the fridge, takes out a plated salad, a pot of cherry yogurt and treats herself to lunch. Gail said chemical digestion of fats starts inside her mouth through the action of enzymes in her saliva. Chewing slowly helps her lingual lipase and phospholipids convert her fats into small droplets. She eats, masticating, chewing slowly, savouring each morsel, pretending that she is a prisoner on death row enjoying her last supper.

Afterwards, she slides the plate into the dishwasher, recycles the yogurt pot, brews herself a verdant fusion of mixed organic peppermint, spearmint and field mint tea leaves then goes to bed. Flipping her i-phone open, she stares at two side-by-side colour photos of Gail: the first taken before, the other taken after, injecting the serum.

Why did she choose to pose topless to show the changes in herself? What did she hope to achieve?

Vicki decides to ring her with all the exciting news, anyway, surprised when Gail accepts her call:

'Hiya, it's only me,' she says, ' Weighed myself just now. Would you believe I lost four pounds?!'

Gail sounds distinctly underwhelmed, 'Only last week you managed to put on five. Listen to me. We need to get your body mass under control: low calorie diet, regular intensive exercise, lots of fluids, for the injections to work.'

'I've joined my local gym,' she informs Gail proudly, 'I've started a daily food diary.'

'Your weight's see-sawing. We need to stabilize you: no fluctuations. I am increasing your serum to two injections a day. How much stock do you have left?'

'About a month's.'

'I'll email you an invoice. Pay me by PayPal. I'll send you enough serum and sharps to last three months. We'll get all that ugly fat off you yet, okay? You can do this. Cross the t off. Don't give up on me, or else.'

Gail makes it sound like a threat: don't give up on me, or else what? which makes her really upset.

'I won't! I won't give up!' she cries at her, wretched and extremely humiliated, 'Thank you, Gail.'

They end their less than friendly chat when Vicki presses eleven different digits on her keypad.

A younger woman's voice, rounded, more pleasant, answers this time, 'Hello, who is it, please?'

'It's me. Is that Eva?'

'You!' Eva giggles, child-like, ever so young for twenty-seven, dresses her horse up as a unicorn, for kids and mum's fairy parties, 'Guess what? It's the kids half-term! I'm doing another party!'

'Don't tell me, you're doing another unicorn party?'

Eva sounds embarrassed, and quietens, 'Mm, it's a *fairy* unicorn party. What can I do you for?'

'Any chance I can order cheeses, humous, pitta, olives and halloumi for two for Valentine's Day?'

'Might be able to fit you in.'

'You're a real star, Eva.'

She feels for Eva, struggling to rebuild her bar trade. The bar is only half-full on the busiest nights of the week let alone in midweek. Eva speaks impatiently. The stress in her voice says it all: she's flying solo again tonight: chief server, head cook, only barmaid, sole bottle washer, 'What time?'

'Tennish.'

'You do know we close at eleven?'

'Don't worry it won't take long.'

It? Not we? Just it? Eva thinks to herself, somewhat baffled, 'Sure, see you Tuesday, then.'

The phone dies. Vicki slinks into bed and checks her messages. There is a new text - from Keira:

Hey, thanks for your daily diet plan. Please Vicki, don't call it a fat plan. You're not fat, just slightly overweight that's all. Never *ever* be ashamed of your body. Well done losing four pounds! Keep it up! I'd love to join you for a glass of wine and bite to eat, thank you. Just one though. Got to drive home afterward. See you Tuesday night, then, Keira.

Vicki sleeps like the dead when she's happy. When she wakes up it's dark outside, intense rainfall drums heavily on her window, a wind is gusting. She screws her face up into a masque and studies her luminous digital alarm clock, 'Six-forty? Can't believe I slept that long. Must be the protein.'

Gail said protein leaves her feeling full. This helps her body to relax, aiding a good night's sleep. By now the fat from her cold sausage salad will be partially digested inside her stomach by gastric lipase as her tummy contracts, converting some of her fat into diglycerides, or fatty acid globules. Most of it will be broken down in her small intestine where the process intensifies and her liver releases bile containing lecithin and bile salts, emulsifiers that break down even more of her fat. Bile, Gail said, grabs her fat and emulsifiers increasing their surface area and making it easier for her enzymes to act on her fats and break apart her fatty acids. Lipase from her pancreas further digests her fat into monoglycerides and fatty acids before her bile again grabs her fat so that it can join with her cholesterol, phospholipids and proteins to form lipoproteins. It is these lipoproteins that enter Vicki's lymphatic system as her gut releases them into the bloodstream for distribution around her entire body.

On that note, she has an unfortunate tendency to accumulate excess fat in her belly, breasts, thighs, arms, hips and buttocks. She vividly recollects Gail's personal plan for her, specifically devised to stabilize, rectify, and slash her body's fat levels:

Make sure you inject yourself same time every morning. If you do miss an injection take it later.

Eat a low-fat diet. Stay off sausages, pizzas, cheese, cream, burgers. Don't give in to temptation.

Eat healthy fats: avocado, nuts, coconut oil, fresh fish.

Protect your liver! Don't drink. If you must, drink only small amounts – no more than two glasses of wine a week.

Join the gym. Get lots of exercise – at least five times for half an hour every week.

Stay in touch. Let me know how it's going.

Alright?

Gail.

flab

The scarlet satin gown with the golden dragon emblazon is hanging on a brass hook on the wall. She yawns, stretches, crawls out of bed, slips it on and pads to the kitchenette barefoot. The chill of the terracotta slate tiles rapidly restores her senses. Until the next online delivery, eating options are limited to organic apple bran yogurts, squash, bananas, flame raisins and a bland crispbread with pumpkin seeds and oats overspread with a low-fat margarine and high-salt vegetarian extract.

She makes up a tray, collects Keira's notes, and lopes off to bed, reading fitness goals as she eats:

S	weight loss: four pounds, one pound a week.
M	measure weight every two weeks.
A	add another session at the gym.
R	relevant enough to implement the changes that are needed.
T	one to four weeks.

Go on Vicki, smash it!

Keira x

Sealed with a Valentine's kiss? As Vicki inputs the data for light supper on her tablet, her stomach rumbles its protest at her perceived lack of sustenance, the paucity of meat. Bored, she slings the device at the bed, gets up, brushes her teeth (she always brushes her teeth after eating), sits in the shower and rests, conserving her energy for the sleepless night ahead. Since resorting to Gail's treatment, her body has been plagued by numerous ailments including bladder pain, cloudy urine, painful, frequent, urination, joint pain, feeling overtired, and worst of all an edgy, rapid heartbeat.

She puts her symptoms down to being fat.

When she saunters into the gym, Keira, resplendent in a tight red women's curved sports bra and matching fitness pants, is busy cleaning under an aerobic cross trainer. Her straggly gingery-red hair is strewn all over her shoulders. Suits her. Vicki admires the bare pale midriff, trim waist and slender physique. She waits while the fitter girl tows her smiling vacuum cleaner out of sight to its little cubby-hole then returns with their mats. Keira throws them on the floor by her box, sits cross-legged in the lotus position, and smiles: a warm, really care about you, kind of smile. Patting the spare mat affectionately as if it's a toy poodle she asks her eager client to, 'Come sit with me.'

Taking care not to show her too much flab, Vicki pulls her cream hoodie over her head, flashing her tummy, sheds her trainers and flops all over the sanitized rubber mat.

'Sorry I upset you the other night,' she says.

Keira shrugs her skinny shoulders, 'No worry. Thanks for the nice post. It was kind of you. Open your heart to me, sweetheart.'

'I find fifteen kilos too heavy when I do the leg curls,' she tells her, 'They hurt my knees. I strain my back on chest press. But I'm thrilled with the progress I've made: my muscles, fitness, stamina levels, energy levels, diet, sleep, attitude, they're all…'

'Great!' adds Keira, reaching behind her back to pull out a laminated double-sided sheet of paper.

Her face is kindly, well-meaning, benevolent. It occurs to Vicki that she might really care about her, maybe more than care. Her voice chimes like happy bells in her mind when the girl whispers in her ear.

'I made this for you.'

She smiles at the handwriting: it's big, bold and easy to read. The sheet is titled Vicki Jayne Hart and sets out her revised exercise and stretches regime: easy line circuits, rower, lateral pulldowns, lateral row pulls, bike, leg curls, leg extensions, abdominal crunches, plank, Russian twists with medicine ball, mountain climbers, bridge, side planks. The chest press isn't mentioned at all and the fifteen kilo leg curl has been reduced to ten kilos. She's struck dumb, speechless. She doesn't know what to say.

Judging by the look of eager anticipation on Keira's face there is even more excitement to come.

She produces a crinkled page of drawings, 'Won't you take a sneaky peek at my matchstick men?'

Having expected at least colour photos, Vicki nearly dies when she sees the silly little spider men performing their spindly leg curls, wiggly straight-line plank and squashed-up apostrophic twists.

'They're amazing!' she laughs, trying hard not to snort, 'Where did you learn to draw like that?'

'Would you believe, infant school?'

Keira asks her to practice three thirty-second bursts of twelve reps on leg curl with ten kilos while she unwraps a chocolate-coated protein bar, gobbling it all up in seconds. Puffed-out, Vicki stares in silence at the white-faced clock above the exercise bikes: it is starkly white - like Keira's flesh.

'If you've no more questions, I think we should leave. Gym shuts in five minutes,' her waif says, standing as gracefully as a doe rising from her bed of dead forest leaves, without using her hands.

Vicki hauls herself up off the floor and follows her to core zone where they spray their mats with sanitizer and hang them on metal wall hooks to dry off. Keira steps inside the cupboard to change reappearing in a sexy dusky pink fake fur-lined hoodie. They hold hands for the first time. Keira's hands feel tender, soft and warm. She respects Vicki. She's proud of her. Pleased for her. She waits while her client visits the women's locker room to freshen up and change, then, leaving the gym behind them, they step out into the mild wet windy night. Her spine tingles as a hand tightens round hers in an erotic restraining tourniquet: Vicki's!

'Frightened, Keira?'

'Why should I be frightened?'

'Thought you might be frightened of the dark, that's all.'

'I'm sure you'd look after me if I was, darling.'

Darling? No-one ever made Vicki feel this wanted. Her heart rises up her throat. Her eyes glisten. They pass through the shadowy swaying pines surrounding the car park, bracing their faces at the rain, skins aglow, heartfelt warmth spreading inside. A battered black Polo occupies the parking slot nearest the exit. Its roof is spattered with wet pine needles. It looks as if it hasn't been washed for weeks. The windscreen is liberally smeared with white bird excrement. That must be my brat's car, she tells herself, smiling.

Keira doesn't know what to make of her. She seems a nice girl, but why does she have to take life so seriously? And the way she spoke to her in the gym. So rude! As if she were her personal slave. As for her looks, her sex appeal, she's dated better-looking girls. It might help if she cheered up. And yet, she has those pretty moles dappling her cheeks, mottling her scalp, that make her look adorable, those sad eyes, that hound-dog expression, the dry-cracked lips, Keira so wants to kiss.

She stops assessing her date, draws a golden packet out of her hoodie, cups her hands, slips a slim black cigarette between her lips and lights up. Its incandescent tip yields a rich red gleam in the gloom, as rich and red as the rosewood rouge she dabbed on her lips when she hid from her buff in her cubby-hole. According to Vicki's application form she doesn't smoke. That doesn't mean, she can't be tempted. Maybe, she just hasn't been offered yet?

Her dead mammy Dawn smoked, occasionally for pleasure, she said. As a child Keira was always finding spent butts in the flower bed whenever she dug for hidden treasure at their weather-beaten, thatched cottage in the woods. Then there were the home-baked cheese scones with butter, cream, jam, afternoon tea at three. Her triple gins and tonic at six. None of mammy's sins seemed to have the slightest effect on her health or beauty. At the age of fifty-seven, she looked youthful. She had a number tattooed inside her left wrist to commemorate her age when her husband Cyd died in a cycle collision with an artic truck, the same year that Keira entered the world. Dawn stunned her friends with her skin-tight pale lemon summer dress when she went to singles parties in search of a new partner in life. Then she fell ill. She died of lung cancer in a hospice six months later. Keira knows that she shouldn't really smoke but can't help herself.

Her lover is giving her creepy looks from underneath her dripping cape: her hooded angel of death waiting to pounce?

'You smoke?' Vicki asks her, casually, not wishing to sound overly judgemental of her girlfriend.

She wipes the fine mist of rain off her sallow cheeks with her free hand, 'Why, are you surprised?'

'Not surprised. Just curious. What with you being so fit and all.'

'Smoking keeps me trim, slim. It stays my appetite. Helps me stay calm. Here, try it,' Keira takes the cigarette out of her mouth, revealing its red ring of lipstick. She hands it to her girl who slips it into *her* mouth, accepting it willingly, without trouble, inhaling then exhaling smoke as if she'd smoked all her adult life, then lights a fresh one for herself, 'Shall we go, then? I'm getting wet.'

They leave the car park huddled against the cursing wind and rain and cross the empty lane that leads to Main Street, passing a social club where neighbours used to gather and smoke, drink, eat plain crisps with navy blue salt sachets, watch sport on tv, listen to bands play, chat, have fun.

Is it any wonder there are so many depressed, lonely, solitary girls searching for someone to love?

Like Vicki.

taste

Eva's of Main Street is a women's bar meaning its décor, furniture, discreet alcoves, fine artwork and music are designed exclusively for women. The menus are pink, garnished with pressed roses and red silk ribbons tied in pretty bows. The lights are dim to accentuate the candles as they flicker in their wax-run, recycled, dusky pink glass bottles, and the music is definitely female: Tina, Kate, Chrissie. The three, cosy, fireside hearths, set deeply into the alcoves, are strung out with vaguely avian-inspired signs: Hen Coop, Bird's Nest, and Chick's Hole.

The girls stub their cigarettes out with their feet and go inside. They are greeted by an empty wine bar, clear polished tables and an exhausted-looking girl dressed in a black, low-cut, deep, ruched evening dress which (more than adequately) shows off her plate flat, bronze, tanned breasts. Vicki is most impressed.

'Hot tan!' she cries, enthusing over the manager's boyish chest and abdomen, 'Love the dress!'

'Got it on my holidays in Italy,' Eva says warily, 'Does it fit me alright? Not too revealing, is it?'

'Suits you with that delicious tan. If you ask me, you look stunning.'

The owner swivels on her heel, 'Sorry, do I know you?'

'I'm Keira. I work as a personal fitness trainer at the sports centre round the corner in Side Street?'

Eva perks up sensing a sexual connotation behind the word delicious, 'Great to meet you, Keira.'

With her frizzy, curly dusky gold-bronze hair, teak eyes, prominent beauty mole on her left cheek, turned-up nose, baby lips and tanned features, she looks as beautiful as a classical realist portrait. Keira is instantly smitten with her, wishing she could paint her nude, loosely draped in her fallen dress, on canvas. Just her, reclining on her lounger. On their own. Oh well, one day. In her dreams.

'Whereabouts in Italy did you go?' she asks.

'Amalfi. It's lovely and hot. You really should go there. Now, where would you guys like to sit?'

'Chick's Hole would be nice.'

'Chick's Hole's free, there it is, then,' Eva points out two tastefully upholstered olive chairs and a round glass-topped cocktail table beside a blazing log fire, beneath a pink Chick's Hole sign, 'What can I get you guys to drink?'

Vicki squeezes her girl's chilled hand. Gail said thin girls feel the cold more than fat girls as they have less blubber under their skin to keep them warm. She stares into an antiquated mirror adorned with etched red roses hanging beside the hearth. Keira's flame-red hair has turned a dark cupric shade from where the rain splashed her face. Her hairline is receding surprisingly quickly for a young woman leaving her with a prominent deathly pale expanse of lightly spotted forehead over her eyes. Bald patches of flaking skin are clearly visible through her thin whorls of hair. Her eyes are bloody lined with ugly grey blotches. Keira doesn't just look exhausted. She looks gravely ill.

Wonder if it's all the smoking? Maybe, if I care for her, love her, nurse her, she'll get better soon?

'Keira?' she adds out loud.

Her brat shivers as a stray raindrop trickles down her spine, 'Do you have any Sauvignon Blanc?'

'Large or small?'

'Small, please.'

'You?'

'I'll have a large glass of Malbec... thanks.'

'One small white, one large red, then,' Eva returns with their glasses of wine, leaving them their obligatory complimentary dish of dry roasted peanuts.

Keira takes off her hoodie, shakes her hair, and makes herself comfortable by the roaring log fire, still wearing her sports bra, revealing her slender lolly stick arms and flat midriff, reminding Vicki how her body could look in three months' time if she doesn't stray from the prescribed game plan.

'This is nice,' she tells her, picking selectively at the stale salty nuts, 'Do you come here often?'

Vic sips her wine appreciatively, 'Only when I'm celebrating special occasions like meeting you.'

Her brat blushes, reaches across the table and touches her wrist. Eying the dish of nuts, Vicki lets her free hand stray until her fingertips are stroking the free fat offerings. She pulls it away, just as Eva is rounding the corner armed with the cheese sharing platter, loaded bowls of baked halloumi fingers, a vase of humus presented with pitta bread slashed into ribbons, a kilner jar full of stuffed olives drenched in herb oil, a clutch of cocktail napkins. She spreads it over the table, withdrawing silently, leaving the starry-eyed lovebirds to enjoy their meal, admire each other, and hold hands.

Keira's immediate concern is: how serious is my girl about losing weight? Laid out before her are fatty slithers of Port Salut, fat chunks of smoked Applewood, sweating wedges of Stilton, melting blocks of ripe Brie, pommes frites of halloumi: a veritable feast of fattening cheeses. She sips her wine and tries to make sense of it all. If she adds in the digestive biscuits, butter, humus, pitta and olives, there is far too much food here for them. Enough for four. The thought of eating all this rich food while millions around the world starve she finds repulsive. She feels conflicted. Feels she should say something, political. Instead, she helps herself to two thick scraps of mouldy blue cheese rind, a scoop of olives, three fat halloumi fingers and half a fresh fig. As her bird swoops, alighting on the residual cheeses like a starving gannet.

Keira eats all of her cheeses, polishes off her wine, relaxes then admits: the food tasted delicious.

'Happy Valentine's,' her sweetheart is saying, slurring, merrily, tipsily, 'Have some more wine,'

'Can't. I'm driving,' Keira protests, 'Got to be up early for work. I'm on mornings.'

Vicki looks over her head as if seeking divine inspiration from someone in the dark, 'Course, you can. No such thing as can't. Cross the t off. Where d'you live? Near here?'

A dribble of red wine runs out of the corner of her mouth onto her chin. Instinctively, Keira takes a clean mouchoir and leans forward, dabbing her shiny skin, her moles, clean, treating her like an infant child who just messed her face. She grabs her wrist, holding her still, gazing into her dreamy eyes. Keira feels the candle's heat, her heat, sear her bare forearm. Wants to kiss her on the lips, can't: she's out of reach, distant. Her spell fades. Her mistress releases her hand. The searing heat recedes. Keira returns to earth.

'I live alone, Holm Wood, ten minutes,' she slurs, after a while, ' Can't afford to lose my licence.'

Eva appears at their table, her black robe makes her look like a sour witch, 'Is everything alright?'

'Everything's perfect,' Vicki says, thirstily, 'Just perfect. Can we have some more wine, please?'

'Sure, same as last time?'

'Just bring us the bottles, will you? And the bill.'

'As you wish.'

Eva fetches two bottles of wine, tops up their glasses, leaves their bill, leaves them alone, leaves them to gaze into each other's eyes across the stained teak table, leaves them so she can clear up in the kitchen.

taste

Resigned to her fate, Keira slumps in her chair, the fire's heat scalding her face, her cheeks flushed flame red.

As her lover leans forward.

And blows her burning candle out.

Lovers

It's late, well after eleven, when they finally leave the bar. Gail stressed the importance of learning how to distinguish between appetite and hunger. Vicki clearly hasn't learnt else her body wouldn't be in the mess it's in tonight. Gail stressed, hunger could occur whenever her tummy was full, or satiated, even if her brain is sending messages to her stomach to say so. If hedonic hunger struck, it could override her brain's authority over eating, her willpower even when she is feeling bloated.

Menu variety stimulates an increase in food intake, apparently. Something different to eat? Such as cheeseboard, humus, pitta, olives, biscuits and a bottle of claret? Dopamine is released sending intense pleasure signals to her body.

This explains why dining out tonight left her wanting more food. And yet, she doesn't feel unwell, swollen or discomfited in any way. On the contrary, she is high as a hot air balloon, euphoric, on dopamine and wine and hasn't felt this happy for ages. Even the torrential rain and blustery winds can't dampen her spirits. Better still, she has the girl she loves most in all the world all to herself.

Keira's head slumps pleasantly against her motherly breasts as she drags her brat off Main Street.

'Want to kiss you,' she murmurs, slurring at her ever so slowly, delving deeply into her intentions.

They embrace underneath the lamppost on the street corner then they kiss: a long, wet, satisfying kiss that promises, I love you. Once they have caught their breaths they enter Slanted Side Street, passing the closed corner shop, a boarded-up nightclub and a thriving antiques shop for wealthier clientele like her mother, rows of terraced houses, curtains tightly drawn. A middle-aged couple approach them walking their blonde terrier. They look the other way. Relieved when she finally reaches the cul-de-sac, Vicki holds her girl still as she fumbles with her keys, shoulders the door open, flicks on the light, and stumbles inside.

Keira perches bedraggled for her on the edge of the bed while she draws the curtains shut, so they can't be seen by the young widower lurking in the house across the road who always seems to be standing behind the window or weeding the lawn or dead heading his rose bush or trimming his privet hedge, watching her. Shutting his antics out of her mind, Vicki goes and stands in front of her brat who has slouched enticingly across the duvet, her lithe body propped up on her bent frail-looking-yet-strong elbows.

'Let's get you out of those wet things, shall we?' she says, trying to sound all adult and responsible while her tummy performs childish flip-flops and her heart pounds hard as a pagan drum, unable to keep the smirk of luscious excitement off her quivering lips.

Keira's cheeks are streaked with sensual blush, she's finding it difficult to breathe, 'I'd like that.'

'Sit up straight then,' her mistress says, voice hoarse, taut, feverish with the thrill of finding love.

'Like a good girl, you mean?' teases Keira, raising a telling brow, her eyes all dreamy, bloodshot.

Vicki's voice falls to a sultry whisper, 'Yes, like *my* good girl.'

Her brat sits up straight for her so that she can ease off her hoodie, winking slyly as she pulls her tight sports bra over her head, up her slender arms. They kiss invasively, infiltrating each other's mouths, unable to restrain their lust. Keira pushes her lover aside, tugs off her trainers and socks, strips off her tight fitness pants and holds her. Vic can smell her putrid flesh. She stinks of cheese, stale sweat. Cherishing an obsession far naughtier than food, she savours her brat's rank, acrid-smelling, pungent, ripe, smoky, cheesy odour inside her nostrils, sighing contentedly.

'My turn.'

Keira stands by the bed, hyper-excited, biting her nails as she strips as far as her pants and bra.

'Want to see your breasts,' she pleads.

Vicki feels behind her back, undoes the fiddly clasp, eases the straps over her shoulders and peels off her underwired cups, freeing her heavy breasts.

'Ah, but they're beautiful, sweetheart,' Keira coos endearingly in a hush voice, 'You're beautiful.'

Her loving words hang in the air between them like thick molten honey rolling out of a honeypot.

Keira wriggles out of her bra then pulls down her pants which are soiled from where she had an unfortunate accident on the walk back from the bar, casually throwing her spoils at the clean fluffy sheepskin bedside rug.

'My poor girl,' Vicki says, stunned by her rude intimate reveal, 'What am I going to do with you?'

Her brat cocks her head to one side naughtily, her spoilt child, 'What do you want to do with me?'

'I want to worship your body.'

Keira squats open-mouthed as her lover slips out of her underwear, revealing her best-kept secret.

'It's my birthmark,' she sighs, pleasurably, before her brat can ask the question, 'Do you like it?'

Keira's finding this hard, 'I do like it, sweetheart, very much so, it reminds me of a smiling face.'

'Do you think so? I never thought of it like that. Perhaps it's a blessing. Lie with me on the bed.'

They lie on the bed exploring each other's bodies - with just the tips of their tongues. Keira worries at the sore weals, myriad punctured holes spread in an obscene rash over her heart's wasted arms, stomach, and thighs. The cruel extent of her lover's self-harm sobers her, 'You inject yourself?'

Vicki rolls onto her side staring at the prepacked suitcase and decides to tell her the truth, 'I inject myself with a serum to reduce my body fat. I found the stuff online.'

It's part of the truth. There's no point mentioning Gail or the control that she has exerted over her life since they met on the train, the squalid details of her obsession with shedding body fat, or the astronomical cost. She doubts Keira will understand, recalling her effusive praise when they met Eva dressed in her revealing dress: if you ask me, you look stunning. She worries, she might lose her. She really needn't worry as Keira is already curling snugly round her body, holding her close, her slender arm wrapped tight around her waist, her heart beating strongly, pounding, offensively, against her back.

'There's no need for you to punish yourself anymore,' she says, 'I'll help you. I *want* to help you.'

'You don't know what this means to me, Keira,' her shoulders heave, she starts to cry, their cheeks touch, their bodies meld, she loves the tickle of spidery fingers crawling along her spine, the soft hand deftly squeezing her ample rump.

'Oh, but I do, sweetheart, I really do. Now, let me kiss away those sweet tears of yours.'

A surge of bliss courses through her veins as Keira kisses her cheeks dry. Her body gives out one of those satisfying little end-of-crying shudders, and she giggles wildly, 'You stink of stale cheese and smoke, love. I really think maybe you should clean your teeth before we have sex, don't you?'

'I think I should,' Keira laughs, 'Wouldn't want my smells to turn you off, darling, would I?'

'You'll find a spare toothbrush in the glass on the vanity shelf under the mirror in the bathroom.'

Keira dismounts her and pads across the gaudy pink glitter twist carpet. Each wall bears a washed out Parisian scene she notices: the

Moulin Rouge, Notre Dame, Eiffel Tower, Arc de Triomphe. The sort of cheap prints you can buy in any cheap tourist shop. Washed-out, like Vicki.

Other than those, the faded sheepskin rug, a mirror and rustic oak dressing table at the foot of the bed, the room is bare. There are no chairs. Presumably, Vicki works in bed? Next to the bathroom door, mounted on a strip of lino, lie the faulty set of scales she uses to fool herself and a pink hard shell suitcase.

She adores her sleeping beauty curled up on the bed, her sad grey eyes closed.

'Planning on going away, sweetheart?' she whispers, softly, 'Planning on leaving me behind?

'Booked a holiday in Amalfi, last week of April, to celebrate losing my fat,' her girl mumbles in her sleep, 'Like to come with me?'

The implications of their shotgun relationship suddenly dawn on Keira. Supposing Vicki doesn't achieve her goal? Supposing she doesn't lose her stone in weight? Then what?

'I'll see,' she tells her in a cautious tone, 'We barely know each other. I'll have to think about it.'

After she has cleaned her teeth and removed all her make-up, she comes back to bed to have sex.

'Don't worry about *your* stench,' she sighs stroking her sleepy lover's lank hair, 'I like you smelly. Lie on your back, sweetheart. Open your legs for me, that's right. Close your eyes, dream of me.'

Vicki, who doesn't wear make-up, admires her brat as she readies herself for her.

'I love your face nude,' she remarks, reaching up to rub her curling lips, 'I love how you call me sweetheart. How you make me feel inside my heart: worthwhile, content, happier than I ever felt.'

'I love you, Keira.'

'And I love you too, sweetheart, very much.'

They kiss then make love with an intense ferocity that defies them to love each other even more. In the small hours, when their lovemaking is spent, they sleep entwined, like babies in the woods.

When Vicki wakes up next morning, Keira has already left.

bloat

Her skin feels hot, clammy and sweaty from where she had sex. Moreover, she can still taste her girl's cheese and smoke, her acrid smell lingering in her nostrils. The bedsheets are crinkled and soiled. They'll need to be washed. As will the pillow case which is strewn with fine ginger-red strands of her Keira's hair.

Vicki smiles at the memories: their intimate kisses, tender caresses. Blows her nose on a crumpled hankie she keeps underneath the pillow and tries to stand. Her head swims, forcing her to collapse, curling inwards, on the edge of the bed, head down, gathering her mind. Once her fuggy brain has cleared, and feeling unexpectedly bloated, she mounts the faulty scales and weighs herself.

'Can't weigh that much, just can't,' she complains.

Her horrid weight gain makes her nauseous. She rushes to the bathroom, kneeling as if in prayer, before the loo, flips the lid, and throws up. Her oily-greasy hair is saturated in sweat. Her eyes are watery: tears of frustration. She flushes away her braque, wipes her runny nose and mouth with a bunched wad of perforated pink toilet tissue then stands unsteadily, gripping the smooth sides of the handbasin, eying the facial mess in the mirror: her cracked lips, welts of tired under her veiny eyes, worst of all: her ghastly moles. Distraught, the living failure clings to Keira's loving words: you're beautiful. They seem alien now, somehow irrelevant.

Once she has flossed, inter-dented, brushed, rinsed and spat the vile titbits out of her mouth, she takes a hot shower, climbs out refreshed, and wraps a soft red bath towel around her waist. Weak daylight filters cautiously past the crack in the curtains. Perspiring heavily, she goes to the dusty dial on the bedroom wall, turns off the central heating, lets her sodden towel fall to the floor, and remounts the scales. Her weight has fallen a little - to just over one hundred and sixty one pounds.

'There,' she sighs, her words riddled with bitter sarcasm, 'That's better.'

She lies on the bed, slides the tip of the needle into the soft flesh of her buttock, and depresses the plunger, purging herself of her ugly fat. At least, that's what the revolutionary solution for rapid fat loss promises to do. If she sticks to her low-calorie diet, takes frequent exercise and controls her hunger pangs, which she can't. Relieved: her purge over, she stills, quietening, rib cage rising, sinking, as she inhales, exhales and slips the cruel metal shard out of her. Rapidly losing faith in life, in her own self-belief, she vents her frustration by hurling the used plastic syringe at the wall.

After changing the sheets and pillow case, she dresses in a khaki jersey top with soft olive lounge pants, ventures as far as the kitchen, drops the syringe in the swing bin, turns the transistor radio on and cooks herself breakfast.

Breakfast is one meal Vicki manages to control. Featuring cooked savouries, pitta and prunes the first day; high fibre cereal, pitta and grapefruit segments the next, it makes up a third of the daily eating ritual she sent Keira on the spreadsheet, the plan she never uses. She remembers her loving words: there's no need for you to punish yourself anymore, I'll help you, I *want* to help you. But she's past being helped now, inconsolable, lost. What's the point of even trying?

Today's menu is scrawled on a torn-off scrap of blank paper fixed to the fridge door by an enamel magnet her mother bought her at an arts and crafts shop in an old malting mill on one of their rare outings to the coast when her mother was well. A token gift. A joke that soon turned sour. A hand-painted image of a wide-eyed fifties brunette: her eyes transfixed, brows raised, mouth opened, ready to eat a yummy ice cream sundae with a glacé cherry on the top, and a telling caption which reads:

I generally avoid temptation unless I can't resist it.

As usual, the menu sheet is incomplete, lacking any details of menu content, calorific values. She opens the fridge and extracts three eggs, three turkey rashers, a squeezy bottle of rancher's honey barbecue sauce, a bowl of pitted prunes to free her bowels, and an out-of-date carton of oat milk. Is this hunger or is it just appetite? she asks herself, putting an egg and rasher back in the fridge.

The kitchen has all the modern essentials needed for survival: knife rack, cutlery tray, chopping boards, work surfaces, her highchair, electric hob, kettle, wall-mounted grill, toaster, dishwasher, washing machine, and tumble dryer. A cupboard in one corner for cleaning materials, iron, ironing board, a mop, brush and bucket.

She switches on the grill and slides the rashers underneath. Beats the eggs up with a whisk. Heats a frying pan sprayed with six squirts of low fat frying oil until the oil fizzes and smokes. Adds the eggs. Quickly boils the kettle, makes herself a mug of instant coffee made with sweeteners and frothing oat milk, grabs a spoon and devours the prunes. Rashers browned, omelette nearly set, she leaps off her highchair, turns off the grill and hob, slaps her meal on a plate, drowns it all in barbecue sauce, adds liberal twists of black pepper and sea salt from the mills, and wolfs it down.

Her mobile rings.

She answers it, 'Hello, who is it?'

It's her mother.

'They're letting me out for the weekend,' she drones sarcastically in her world-weary drawl, 'I've to be back by eight for supper else I'll be in trouble for being a naughty girl. But there's nothing the matter with me. Is there?'

Vicki doesn't answer, at first. Naughty girl? Nothing the matter? She pictures her mother standing by a sealed window with a wide oak frame, staring out at the dull grey grounds as the rain drizzles miserably down the pane, as it did the last and only time she visited her.

She relives the dreadful moments.

mind

She drove along the narrow country lane taking care to change down for each speed hump in case she got a flat tyre. The track was bordered by bared sweet chestnut trees their rotted leaves turned to slush by the incessant rain. She imagined them squelching beneath her tyres as her Mini slipped and slid. Stressed at the notion of the unknown: her mother's state of mind when they finally met, she struggled to keep her self-control. The car park was overlooked by a well-tended lawn pitted with beds of crimson roses. Crab apple trees groaned at the burden of their heavy fruit. Occasional benches lay vacant, waiting for absent patients to sit on them admiring the view when the weather was fine. It was raining, cats and dogs, the sky overhead was deathly grey with storm clouds, the visitors' car park empty. Undaunted, she parked the car, turned off the Sunday afternoon rock show on the radio, killed the engine and waited for the rain to ease.

In the end, she just made a dash for it.

When she entered the hospital lobby, dripping, her dull mood darkened at the sight of its morbid heavy oak panels. She smelled pear drops, the thick stench of disinfectant. Seeing an arch ahead of her, a brass plate marked Reception, she walked underneath to the opulent surroundings of an exclusive private patients visitor's room. The grey panelled walls were inset with buff alcoves, each of them lit to highlight twisted marble torsos of naked men and women mounted on podia.

At the centre of the room sat an antique inlaid wooden desk bearing a vertical display of books boasting the history of the house, its estate, a brass bell, a brass tent card which read Mila your Receptionist and a pair of ornate tulip lights surmounted dominantly on their moulded, straining, silver stands.

Mila had a ridiculously healthy bronze tan, beautiful golden hair falling as far as her breasts, and a v neck blouse puffed at the sleeves. Her slim hands rested on the desk with her fingers splayed. Her perfect nails weren't varnished. She wasn't wearing a ring. Busy, studying a roadmap, Mila lifted her head, her mouth creasing into a lovely smile, and talked with a plum in her wide mouth.

'Good Afternoon. May I help you?'

'I've come to visit my mother, Mrs Hart,' Vicki said drying her damp face and hair with a scented handkerchief.

'I'm afraid you *are* rather early. It's only four o'clock. Visiting hours don't usually start until five. Might you like to sit in the armchair? Can I get you some coffee while you're waiting, Ms, Miss?'

'It's Ms,' she said, affecting a middle class accent, 'I'd love a cup of coffee. Thank you.'

Vicki made herself comfortable in the plush velvet pink armchair by the roaring log fire, drying off while Mila dispensed a fresh pot of filter coffee from a bean-to-cup machine in one of the alcoves, leaving the tray on the glass-topped table by the fire. Loving the feeling of being spoilt, she helped herself to coffee, cream from a silver jug, brown sugar, plus three rich coated chocolate biscuits, then she sank deep-and-low into the welcoming womb of the springy armchair, shut her eyes and slept.

An hour later, she was gently nudged awake by Mila. A well-built, cheerful, African male nurse called Marcus, dressed in a crisp white smock, went with her to her mother's bedroom. As they trudged the winding threadbare carpeted spiral staircase beneath the glittering fake chandelier, he explained to her that Annette had her good days and bad days but seemed to have been on a more even keel recently. When they reached her bedroom, the nurse let her inside, stood in the doorway, watched and waited.

Annette was wearing the same grey and white striped cheesecloth dress she wore on the night the ambulance ferried her to hospital, standing stiff, her hands clasped tightly under her belly. On her wrist, she bore a number thirty-three tattooed in black.

What's that for? Vicki wondered, then she remembered, the nurse had shown her into Room 33.

The woman twisted her head to face her. Vicki would never forget the anger in her look, the fury in her eyes, the sore, puffy lips pursing, twitching, snarling, blowing out her ironic, spiteful words, 'Well, look what the rain just washed in.'

She studied her smart court shoes, 'Sorry I didn't come to see you, mummy. I've been so busy.'

'Busy? Sorry? I should think you *are* sorry. I've been locked in here for months. Max visits me, *religiously*,' her mother said, emphasizing the word for effect, 'Every Sunday evening. You know how busy *he* is, Victoria.'

She did know, full well, how busy her brother: purveyor of luxury animal-friendly biodegradable men's fragrances, barrier cream and skin lotions, was. Busy, securing his claim to sole inheritance of his mother's six-bedroom country manse on the outskirts of Meerten, where he lived, and all her considerable wealth. She imagined him, the favoured child, sitting on the bed with his vacant parent, holding hands, watching the minutes click by on her Barbie Returns clock until it was time for him to leave.

'I bought you some chocolates,' she said, quietly, changing the subject, 'They're wafer thin mints, your favourites, and some nice roses.'

She took the chocolates out of a dark green plastic M&S carrier bag, holding out the flowers as if they were her olive branch, a peace offering to make up for her being such an unloving daughter.

Annette suddenly exploded, 'I don't want your bloody charity! I'm not ill. I want to go home!'

In her foul maddened rage, she ripped the flowers out of her child's hands, tearing the cellophane, throwing them on the floor, scattering petals, leaves, thorny stems, over the warm beige stainproof carpet, stamping on them, frenziedly, with her bare feet, cutting herself to shreds without noticing.

Vicki was terrified. She started crying, shouting. She screamed at her, 'Stop it, mummy! Stop it!'

'Give me those!' her mater roared, wrenching the black box from her grasp, clawing the wrapper, throwing mints around, like chocolate dominoes, over her chequered-patterned continental quilt, over the plain emulsion primrose wall, over her daughter who bawled, 'Those chocolates cost me five pounds, mummy!'

Marcus pressed a red alarm button next to the door, summoning urgent aid. 'Your mother's having a bad episode,' he gabbled, 'I think it's best you leave. Don't worry, we'll look after her.'

Annette turned hysterical, clutching the nurse's sleeve, pleading for him to let her daughter stay: 'Please, don't make her leave me! I love her! I love you, Victoria! Don't leave me here, darling!'

Badly shaken, Vicki shied off through the open door. Just as two male orderlies approached armed with hypodermics primed with blue fluid. Her mother's screams spread like plague to all the other patients who moaned and groaned, pined and whined. Soon, the air was ripe with the shrill, craze-tangled birdsong of the ill, the depressed, the clinically insane.

When she did manage to escape into the outside air, her hands were shaking hard. The fresh chill of the autumnal rain brought her back to her senses. She tried to rationalize her mother's irrational behaviour vowing not to return to the secure mental health unit hidden in the chestnut trees again.

On the long drive home, she pulled into the nearest petrol station, took herself a family-size block of fruit and nut chocolate, a grab bag of cheese and onion crisps, a greasy sausage roll, a tube of soft chewy spearmints, then she sat, in the car, broken, shattered, and consumed it all in minutes.

challenges

'How are you feeling now, mummy?' she asks her, tentatively.

'I'm fine. The doctors are very pleased with my progress. I might be coming home for good soon.'

Her voice fades then mellows, saddened by her forlorn hope of freedom. Vicki feels sorry for her mother, and yet, inside, she thinks, I hope not. I mean what's the point? She'll only have another episode and have to go back in again. She tries to shake off the nagging doubts and listen to what her mother is saying.

'Max has planned a homecoming celebration for me on Sunday: afternoon tea at a hotel in the West End. He is collecting me from here on Friday night. Taking me home. Then, on Saturday, we're off to Trés Jolie to buy me a new outfit. Then it's out to dinner at Charades. Oh darling, I'm so thrilled to be out of that place. You *will* join us on Sunday, won't you, Victoria? Before I have to go back...'

Back. Inside that dreadful hospital. Vicki wonders when Keira has her days off? Must she work this weekend? She thinks of all that rich food: sandwiches, cakes, scones with clotted cream, fine fruit jams. Max showing off, quaffing glass after glass of imitation champagne.

Gail warned her that she would face challenges when she went out: 'Make sure you cut right back when you get home afterward. Just a light healthy salad, a piece of fruit and lots of water to drink.'

'Of course, I will,' she says.

'Good! I've asked Max to WhatsApp you with the arrangements. I love you, Victoria.'

'Love you too, mummy,' she whimpers, setting the phone down beside her empty breakfast plate.

She sits on her highchair sipping lukewarm coffee, reflecting on how fortunate she is: to be able to do whatever she wants, come and go where and whenever she pleases, have someone to love: Keira. Trapped inside the mental health unit, plied with medication, restraining fluids, her mother is little more than a caged laboratory animal waiting to be treated, conditioned and assessed to see if she is safe to be let out, yet. Vicki resolves to be much kinder towards her only parent in future.

Her dirty gym gear, underwear and the bed linen lurk in an untidy heap on the floor. She gathers it all up in her arms and stuffs it in the washing machine, setting the wash to eco-mix, to save the planet. There's a light knock on the door. With all the recent changes in her life, she forgot to buy a new battery for the doorbell. More knocks, but louder this time. The kitchen's in its usual sordid state. She stashes her dirties in the dishwasher and slams the door. A repetitive pounding, this time, on her only way out. Barefoot, mind-in-a-tizz, she rushes through the bedroom, and unlocks the door.

He is standing, motionless, in the pouring rain. The young man from across the road. The widower with the red and black rose-cutting secateurs and turquoise electric hedge trimmer. Her torso gives an involuntary shiver. He is holding an express delivery package, a bulging, buff jiffy bag sealed at one end with transparent tape. He holds it out in front of him. For her to take.

'I think this is meant for you,' he says, coldly, dispassionately. There isn't any cheer in his voice.

She reaches forward to take it. He snatches it back from her. She can see, he's really tried for her this time. Changed his appearance since they last met. Had his hair blow-waved in a quiff. Grown a neatly trimmed beard, a distinguished smattering of grey hairs on his chin. It suits him, makes him look younger, almost handsome. His clothes look as if they are all brand new: Fatface, John Lewis? He's wearing a black and grey woven herring-bone sweater, dun buttons, high neck at the back, a small v neck under his throat. She can just make out his chest hair. The olive chinos are well-hung, pristinely pressed and he's wearing tanned leather moccasin slippers stained umber by the rain. Getting wet. She can't understand why he doesn't just hand her the parcel and leave.

'Aren't you going to invite me in?' he says without looking her in the face, scrutinizing her body.

Underneath her thin jersey she isn't wearing a bra. She feels naked. He can see her nipples, jutting, through the clingy, thin material.

'I saw you getting fresh with her last night,' he says, 'Thought you might be in need of a man.'

'Get lost!'

'As you wish.' He throws the bundle at her midriff. She catches it, steps inside. He makes a grab for her wrist, misses. Upset, scared by him, she slams the door in his face. Safe. At least, for now. Once she has steadied her frayed nerves, recovered and fully dressed, she opens the parcel. Inside are twelve bubble-wrapped phials of serum, an invoice marked PAID, and a typed line from Gail:

I think we should meet urgently to review your progress.

Call me,

Gail.

Carefully, she unwraps each bottle, placing them in the jiffy bag, goes to the bathroom, opens the mirror-fronted cabinet above the toilet, and arranges them on the glass shelf. Mulling over Gail's latest assault, she makes herself a fresh mug of coffee then sits in her highchair, revolving, reliving the moment they first met.

Tease

Her teeth were sacrosanct, meaning they were much too important to her to be damaged, stained, decayed, changed, replaced or altered in any way. She was prepared to tolerate permanent welts of tiredness underneath her haggard eyes, the obscene bulb at the end of her nose, her dry, cracked lips, even her unsightly moles, all of which could be removed with invasive cosmetic surgery. But not bad teeth. Having clean, bright, shiny teeth gave her a quaint smile which in turn made her feel better inside her mind and body, at least, while she was still fat. Vicki actively looked to protect her teeth, treating them as if they were rare metal jewels, constantly brushing them, caring for the gums that encased them so they didn't rot, decay then fall out.

Having failed to find a dentist who would take her on in Main Street or Off Street, she plumped for a private dentist and hygienist in Soho, paid for out of her savings. Twice a year, she took the train to London, walked half a mile to the impressive, converted brothel, had her teeth cleaned by delightful Carmen, the cheerful hygienist from Jamaica, then inspected by Lara the sterner dentist from up-and-coming Hackney. Her examination took an hour. Desperately searching for someone to talk to, she seized every opportunity to converse with them both, whenever her mouth was free.

Afterwards, she treated herself to a bottomless brunch and half a bottle of prosecco at Bill's before slumping in the back seat of a pre-booked Uber cab back to Elting, her self-inflated obesity, and loneliness.

The station was a good ten minute walk downhill from her cul-de-sac. She crossed Main Street at the lights, passing the Shell garage with it's tempting Little Waitrose, a boarded-up ground floor bar, some ultramodern apartments then took Hill Street past the vets, a care home and a sand pit. Until she reached her short cut: a shady concrete staircase surrounded by high fences draped in brambles and ivy. She took a deep breath, tightened the amber scarf around her neck and coughed.

The air today felt cool, damp and foggy, the ground was covered with a thick mulch of leaf mould, dead blackberries, rotting russet husks of apples. Rats thrived here at this time of year, she knew, fat, cider-drunk, rats that urinated on the path. She trod firmly on each step so as not to slip and fall, imagining the state she'd look if she arrived at Lara's covered in detritus.

Having negotiated the treacherous steps, the station was just a short half circuit of the mucky tarmac park around the perimeter fence of the car park. Vicki crossed the busy station approach covering her mouth with her hands as she passed a smoke chundering bus.

Why doesn't the bus driver turn the engine off? she questioned, churning all that filthy dirt out into my airspace, polluting my lungs.

There were no free Metro's left for her to read in the newsstand so she slipped a hand inside her long padded coat with white wool trim and hood and took out her debit card. She kept her cards concealed inside lustrous silvery STOP RFID THEFT pouches to prevent the scammers from stealing her details. She entered the station. The ticket hall was full of impatient travellers waiting for the peak travel period to end at nine thirty. Would she catch flu or Covid, despite having had the Moderna booster given to her in September by the friendly Asian male chemist, in his dinky clinic in Main Street?

She held her breath, gasping hard when she spotted a stunning young woman with flouncy ginger hair, freckled face, shimmering glossed lips, and piercing ash-grey eyes. She couldn't stop staring at her. The woman raised her brows and gave her a gorgeous why-not-come-over-and-talk-to-me smile. Could she be the role model she had been searching for since she visited her ill mother in hospital? Vicki wished she could look like her. Minutes passed. Peak period ended. Beguiled, she walked through the automatic gates and made her way along the platform to an empty carriage at the far end of the train. Sat close to the exit, coat unbuttoned to reveal her white pierced cotton vest and autumnal printed midi-skirt.

All her dreams came true when the redhead in the waxed olive jacket, leather miniskirt and knee-length boots sat next to her. Their thighs touched. They twisted in their seats and faced each other. They broke into natural smiles at the same time.

The woman with the freckled face said, 'I saw you staring at me. Why were you staring at me?'

Words tumbled out of her mouth like love hearts out of a sweetshop jar, 'You're beautiful. I'm just fat and ugly.'

'Listen, never be ashamed of your body or how you look,' the ginger said, forcibly in her opinion, 'You've a beautiful face, a lovely figure. And you're definitely not fat.'

'I'm always tired. My back hurts. I sweat hard. I'm fat. I can't seem to lose weight.'

'I can help you change,' the woman undid her jacket, drew out a silver cardholder, flipped it open and passed her a crisp, snow-white business card inscribed with the name, Gail Murragh, and title, Fatness Consultant, embossed on the front in raised gold lettering, 'Give me a call, won't you?'

Before Vicki could speak, the driver announced that the train was about to leave, the doors hissed shut, and the train set off. They left the town behind, gliding under a bridge, passing through bland fields of churned mud, sowing fanciful seeds in her mind. Gail slumped asleep on her shoulder. The elderly couple sitting opposite sagged in their seats, their wrinkled chins fallen to their chests, lost in a slumberland of distant memories, oblivious to the onslaught of the harsh, outside world.

She smelled the fresh fragrance of Gail's hair, the subtle hint of roses on her cheeks. Felt her slim body press against hers. She was feeling aroused and wasn't sure she could help herself. Her prey was only wearing a flimsy camisole top underneath her jacket. Gently, she slipped her hand inside her lacy bra cup and caressed her puffy breast.

'That feels lovely,' Gail sighed contentedly, 'Touch me, down there. Go on. Don't be shy.'

Intoxicated by her tease, heady with lust, she felt the softest, barest flesh beneath her miniskirt…

ruse

Vicki could kick herself for having been cuckolded by Gail, falling for her sexual ruse. She studies the thin slip of paper that came with her medication: the obscene cost of a further three months of painful obsession: double the dose, double the price. For what? A lifetime of false hope, fruitless misery? In any case, she no longer needs Gail, she loves Keira. She tears the invoice to tiny shreds, mixing it with the general waste in her flip-top bin then scrolls through the contacts on her phone and tablet and blocks Gail, removing every trace of her from her life. The dishwasher, which she always sets to Quick 45 to save the planet, beeps, telling her the worst is over.

Resisting the urge to eat a fistful of lemon curd biscuits from the yellow and turquoise treat barrel she keeps high on a kitchen shelf, she retires to her bed, picks up her latest manuscript, and reads. The author's writing is hard, disrespectful, sexist, yet loving, and utterly compulsive - like him:

He was feeding her soup from a silver spoon, and she loved him. Feeding her like that! The soup was thick and warm, coating her gums and teeth, teasing her glands into salivation, frothing before she swallowed her mouthful. She opened her mouth, licking her raspberry-red lips with the tip of her tongue, craning her head for him, then dropped her jaw so that he could feed her again. She dribbled some, felt the tiniest trickle run down her dimpled chin, but he dabbed her clean with a soft mouchoir, so the soup never reached her neck. She blushed. Her cheeks bloomed with roses.

He stopped feeding her.

ruse

She felt his hand brush her wavy teak hair behind her elfin ear. His fingertips pressed into the line of her parting. Her hair was parted on the left. He ran his hand down her smiling face and felt her straining neck, her vein. She pursed and puckered her lips to kiss him. Their lips touched, lightly at first. Then they kissed. She ran her fingers through his hair. She loved him. They kissed and kissed, as if their lives, their loves, depended.

His hand pressed on her, stroking her chunky gold necklace. He slid his fingertips under her flimsy satin top and caressed her neck and shoulder. She felt his hand grip her tightly, insistently, then heard a voice: vague, distant, coming close, closer. It wasn't his voice. Their lips no longer kissed. He released her. He drifted away. Her mind pleaded for him to stay.

There was birdsong: a dawn chorus. The hum of distant traffic, a car approaching, a bus. Children's laughter, muffled, in a nearby room. A shard of daylight filtered through the tangerine curtains warming her face. She smiled as she felt the soft hand resting on her shoulder, shaking her awake: the sound of her mother's voice, 'It is time to wake up, Marie. Did you sleep well?'

Marie blinked at the sunlight as Maman walked across the threadbare carpet, went to the window, and drew back the gaudy orange curtains sending up a fine mist of dust motes. The window was grubby, soiled with grime off the street, dashed with pigeon droppings. Maman looked down at the statue of Andre Gill the noted cartoonist, standing formally in the middle of the small grey square, then she turned to face her daughter.

'I had the loveliest dream, Maman,' Marie said, pushing herself into an upright seated position with her strong legs, 'I dreamed I fell in love with a man.'

'Ah, but that is a lovely dream, Cheri!'

Maman was very beautiful. Her stunning looks belied her age of fifty. She had soft, round, smiling cheeks. Her blonde hair had been cut into a bob, blow-waved off her face, giving her a youthful, boyish appearance. She was up, dressed in a shabby grey cardigan over a crisp open-neck white blouse and navy jeans. Her sleeves were rolled up to the elbows in readiness for the chores to come. Maman could easily have passed for a woman in her late twenties were it not for the worry-lines etched into her face, the dark blotches under her eyes. She stuffed a hand into her jean pocket, flashed a radiant smile at her daughter, and sagged against the wall propping up her spirits with her outstretched arm. Marie caught the sadness in her eyes and challenged her.

'But I will never fall in love, will I Maman?'

Her mother, looking downcast, fixed her stare on a fat pigeon, squatting on the window ledge. She didn't reply. Marie felt like strangling her when she acted like this, shying from the truth: her terrible imperfections.

She persisted, 'Will I Maman?'

'No, Cheri,' her mother conceded, 'You will never fall in love.'

'But I still have you?'

'Yes, you still have me.'

They lived in a pauper's room, a homage to their poverty, which was sparsely furnished with a chest of drawers, wardrobe, table and chair, a sturdy three-legged stool, and a hand basin. But the walls were daubed with colour, delicate paintings: bright red tulips, yellow chicks, white blossom, azure blue seas, golden sandy beaches, shady harbours, a blood-orange sunset, and smattered here and there on a partially painted canvas, snowdrops.

Marie pushed the duvet off the bed with her feet, swung her legs off the bed, and stood,

'I have to go to the toilet, Maman.'

'Call me when you have finished. Oh, and run a bath for yourself, Cheri.'

Marie nodded and padded across the worn-out carpet to their bathroom while her mother busied herself making their bed. Mother and child had slept entwined in the bed since the fateful day that she gave birth there in front of her beloved husband Georges. She recalled the look of shock on his face, on the midwife's face, when Marie slid too easily from her womb. How Georges burst into tears and stormed out of the room never to be seen again. The midwife staring sorrowfully into her eyes as she cut their cord and passed over her bloodied bundle of joy to Maman for her to hold and suckle, making her apologies, and leaving her to cradle the disfigured baby. That was all in 1960. Today was her daughter's twenty-third birthday. Maman pressed the creases out of the sheet, fluffed up the pillows, and drew up the duvet, admiring the unfinished painting hanging overhead. Her mind was clouded with guilt. Her throat was choked with shame. But her eyes were filled with tears of pride. She sank to her knees and wept for her tarnished child.

Marie closed the bathroom door with her bottom, then pulled at the light cord with her mouth. The place was a dingy hole with thick black mould growing on the window fan and around the bath. She hurried to the window, pulled at the fan cord with her mouth, reached for the bath plug with her left foot, gripping its chain between her toes, and pressed it into the plughole with the sole of her foot. Next, she turned on the hot and cold taps with her toes and went to the toilet. The lavatory was a dark hole in the floor with a wooden seat flush to the ground. Marie squatted over the abyss sighing with relief as she freed her heavy bowel and emptied her swollen bladder. Then she called out to Maman.

'I've finished!'

Quickly, she stood up, reached for the cistern handle with her right foot, and flushed the toilet. Her mother strode in, brown mascara running down her cheeks, tore off a thick wad of soft tissue, gently eased her legs apart, and wiped her bottom, front to back, as if Marie were still her baby. After disposing of the mess, she splashed a little bath foam into the warm water and gestured for her daughter to clamber into the bathtub. Marie knew why her mother had been crying but didn't say a word.

Once Maman had bathed and towel-dried her child they went to the bedroom which was bright, warm and sunny, lit by dusty sunbeams. She fetched the sturdy three-legged stool and placed it in front of the hand basin. Marie sat on the stool, reached up for the loaded toothbrush with her right foot, turned on the cold water tap with her left foot, then cleaned her teeth. Maman stood at her side. She never ceased to marvel at the sheer flexibility in the young woman's toes: her 'fingers,' the supple legs and feet: her 'arms and hands.' As Marie dabbed her mouth dry, she swivelled on the stool to face her mother, delighted, and surprised, to see a smiling, happy, Maman cradling three parcels tied up with pink ribbons in her arms.

'Happy Birthday, Cheri!' she cried, stemming back her tears, 'Shall I put them on the bed for you to open?'

'Oh, Maman! I love you! Thank you! Thank you!'

Maman placed the two flimsy packages on the middle of the bed. Marie hesitated at first.

'Go on then, open them!'

She watched avidly as her daughter squatted on the duvet and tore apart the loose ribbons, pulling off the shiny red wrapping paper with her toes.

'I wonder what they are?' Marie said, grinning from ear-to-ear.

'You'll see! You'll see!'

Marie, who was born partly limb-deficient, well used to wearing old sweaters knotted at the elbows, and Levi's, stared despondently at the beautiful royal blue satin sleeveless top and pleated white skirt lying between her feet. Her mother had dreaded this moment. Had feared her attempt to celebrate Marie's womanhood, her stunning natural beauty, would cause this upset. Ashamed of the actions that she took in all innocence when she was a young woman herself: actions that directly resulted in her daughter's horrid deformities. Wishing the floor would open up and swallow her whole, she braced herself.

'What is it, Cheri?'

Marie lowered her head, so that her chin rested on her chest. Her wavy teak hair fell in a flop over her face. She cried gently. She didn't want to upset her mother by letting her see her cry on her birthday.

Marie hated her body, hated her physical aberrations, hated herself, the human abnormality that she was. Why couldn't she be normal like the other artists?

'I cannot wear these clothes, Maman!' she blurted suddenly, 'You know I can't! Why have you offended me so?'

Marie's harsh words cut into her mother's heart like a bitter sword of hatred. Swallowing her pride, she begged her daughter's forgiveness, explaining to her beloved that she was only trying to make amends. For the mistake she made during her pregnancy. For the drug she took when she lived in England with her husband George (his real name): the Distval, otherwise known as thalidomide.

Maman opened her final present, the small parcel, and withdrew a hard, black jewellery box. She took out the chunky gold necklace and hung it round her crying daughter's neck.

'This was Grand Mere's,' she wept, 'I want you to have it, to wear it for me, always, because you are beautiful, Cheri, because you have nothing to be ashamed of. It is me who should be ashamed.'

She slumped on the bed and held her baby in her tender motherly embrace.

Marie cried, 'Oh, I am so sorry. I love you, my dear, sweet, sad Maman.'

They cried, as one. They shed teardrops.

Snowdrops. Marie painted snowdrops.

With her mouth.

guilt

Vicki detests reading this kind of story. Not because it's badly written, doesn't flow, isn't really a story or lacks sufficient structure. She detests reading his story because she finds it controversial, struggling to remain impartial when she reads it. Sure, there are obvious errors: she suspects the story is set sometime in the early-to-mid-eighties, but she can't be certain. It doesn't have a title.

Her issue, as a woman, is the sexual innuendo alluded to within the text. Was it really necessary for the author to go into explicit detail, describing how the mother wiped her disabled, grown-up daughter's bottom clean after she had squatted over an open toilet?

On the other hand, she loves the candid nature of the story, the statement it makes about the girl's triumph over disability, as a painter without arms, her inner strength, the strained mother-daughter relationship, the devastating legacy of thalidomide.

She wipes away tears from her eyes, moved to crying by the girl's plight, recalling how badly she treated *her* mother, wrought with guilt for not visiting her for months when she was locked away.

One major criticism: the story, like some others in the author's anthology (who buys anthologies these days anyway when you can read short stories online?) is too brief. As the reader, she would like to have known if the girl found love. As she found love with Keira. She props herself up with her pillows and checks the time: ten-thirty, missing her, hoping she will call round to see her after she finishes work. Thank goodness, she has Keira to share her life with, writing to focus her mind.

This is her job, it is what she does, it's what pays the bills. Besides, proof-reading stops her eating. She reflects on how vain she has become, her ever maddening obsession with being fat. Her mind returns to the book's critique. She pens her suggested alterations, comments on its printed pages:

Tone down the sex if you want to sell any books. Your stories are too brief: they need fleshing out, extending, bringing to the acceptable conclusion discerning readers expect. Other than that, there are a few grammar and spelling mistakes. Overall, I think your book is quite well-written.

Such a shame, the author relishes in so much sex, erotica really, when he writes love stories. She considers the challenging project she tasked herself with proofing, formatting, designing a cover, publishing his book: a new direction for her, reflected in a discounted cost to him. She makes a sheaf of the pages ensuring they are arranged in strict numerical order, leaves them on her dressing table, goes to the window and watches the rain fall.

He writes sex for a reason. He told her he was lonely and hadn't had a woman in his life, not since his soulmate died. Her heart goes out to him, recalling how harshly she treated him when she told him, bluntly, where to go. Still, he deserved it – scaring her like that.

It stops raining, leaving the pitted tarmac road spattered with puddles, here-and-there reminders of their encounter in the rain. Her mouth's dry, her tummy rumbles. It's time for elevenses: a glass of blackcurrant squash, a small fistful of flame raisins, to help her make it through to lunchtime.

She licks her lips, contemplating the lemon curd biscuit treats waiting for her inside the cupboard.

She asserts herself, desisting, strides to the kitchen, fetches a glass of water, and sits on the bed readying herself to read his next story. Her concentration is broken when something hits the door. She permits herself a wry smile, singing to herself: the refrain of the song she heard earlier on the radio. She does him a favour, opens the door, and lets him in.

loneliness

He is crying. She has never seen a grown man crying before. The only other man in her life never cries. Ever since their childhoods, Max has been a cold heart: detached, aloof and insensitive: an automaton, an unemotional robot. She supposes that must be how he copes when their mother is ill. Vicki has never met her father. Jim died in a tragic road accident the month after she was born. He went missing during one of her mother's dark episodes. The search team found his body five days later locked inside his car underwater in a swollen river with the driver's window wound down. The coroner declared an open verdict. Her mind asks her conscience if her father cried out for her as he died.

He is wearing the same woven herring-bone sweater, olive chinos and leather moccasin slippers that he wore standing in the rain when he delivered her serum. His clothes are dry. She suspects, he might keep an identical spare set of clothes for emergencies, wouldn't put it past him. Other than his outward appearance, he's in a wretched, broken, dejected state. She takes pity on him.

'I think you should come inside,' she says, standing to one side.

He sees her bedroom, her washed-out prints, sheafs of paper hanging over the edge of her dressing table, sees inside her private sanctuary.

'Nice pad,' he says off-handedly, he doesn't really mean it.

Her converted garage reminds him of the squalid bedsit he rented over a barber's shop in an inner-city slum before he made it as a grill chef, met the love of his life, married her, got promoted several times over, and they moved out to the leafier suburbs.

loneliness

She shrugs her shoulders noncommittal, 'It's all I can afford. At least, I have a roof over my head.'

'I want to apologize for the way I behaved earlier,' he says, 'I was bang out of order. I'm sorry.'

'You frightened me, Alleyn,' she says standing apart from him, wary, still scared, excited, inside.

'I mean it. I'm really sorry.'

Her heart melts, she's never seen him this vulnerable before. His sad demeanour makes her feel needed, wanted. That and the tears streaking his face. She likes the feeling. Finds herself warming to him.

He rubs his sore red eyes, 'My wife died a year ago.'

'A year ago, today?'

'She was killed in a car crash, a year ago this morning.'

'How awful for you.'

'It is – awful.'

Sunlight streams through the door over him creating a halo effect, a pale aura around his head.

Vicki reaches behind him and shuts the door.

'Would you like to tell me about it?' she says, offering herself, 'I find it helps to talk to somebody.'

'It would help me a lot… thanks.'

'I was about to treat myself to a mug of coffee and creamy lemon curd biscuits. Can I tempt you?'

He smiles. His smile makes him look young. It soothes his grief, the pent-up anger at his loss. His woman's premature death was his fault. He confided as much to Vicki when they met to discuss his book of painfully frank love stories - without revealing the reason why.

'Sit yourself down then,' she says softly, 'There's only the bed I'm afraid. I can't fit in any chairs.'

He sits, uneasily, on the edge of the bed staring at her mirror, rubbing his cheeks dry, tidying his hair, 'What's with all the fattening biscuits all of a sudden? You told me you were on a strict diet.'

'I am,' she admits, 'The biscuits are for you. Make yourself comfortable. I'll be back in a minute.'

She returns minutes later with steaming mugs of black coffee, a jug of skimmed milk, sweetener, her best blue and white *Delph* china pot of demerara sugar, and a plate of lemony crunch biscuits which she sets out on a robust tray to prevent spillage on the bed. She sits with the tray between them, marking out their territories as if she is his lynx, or wildcat, and studies him…

'Milk? Sugar?'

'Four sugars, dash of milk.'

A man with a sweet tooth? Sweet tooth or sweet heart? She sprinkles the sugar in his coffee, adds milk then hands him her red mug bearing the inscription: Stay Calm You're Only 27.

He cups it in his hands. She milks her drink. They drink.

'This tastes good.'

She laughs, 'It's instant. Try the biscuits, they're delicious from *Fortnum's,* a present from my bestie.'

He looks at her, mystified, 'Your bestie?'

'My best friend,' she explains, staring at the print of Sacre Bleu on the far wall, 'Her name was Jewel. We met near Place des Artistes in Paris. It was raining outside, pouring. The artists in the square covered their easels and sheltered from the rain. I ran for cover to the nearest bar. I found her there. We talked. She spoke good English. I spoke a little French. We shared a bowl of onion soup covered with melted cheese and drank a lot of rough wine. Afterward, when the rain stopped, she led me to her little room off Moulin Rouge, stripped me, then made the sweetest love to me.'

He feels himself stiffen, 'You make her sound sensual, sexual. You should take up writing, you're a natural.'

loneliness

'She was - sensual. Marie, the girl in your story, reminded me of her emotions, her mannerisms.'

'Except, Jewel has arms to hold you with and Marie didn't, right?'

'Had arms.'

'Had, not has?'

'Had. The next day, I returned to England. We wrote each other letters, became pen pals, besties. Sent each other gifts: biscuits, cheese, chocolate, flowers, that sort of thing? Jewel always told me we should meet, here, or in Paris. I never found the time. In the end, she stopped writing.'

'Sorry, I'm not being much help, am I?'

'Not at all, I like talking to you. I've had no-one to speak to since Lucy died,' his voice falters, 'You wouldn't believe how lonely I get living in that big house without her.'

'I would,' she says, staring into empty space, 'I get lonely, too.'

love

They sit in silence.

After helping herself to all the biscuits, she takes his empty mug, lifts the tray, and places it on the floor.

Vicki inches nearer to him, 'I liked the story very much, the statement it made, Marie's triumph as a mouth painter, her strength of character, the strained mother-daughter relationship, the tragic effect of thalidomide. I have some feedback on how you can make your writing accessible to readers. That's if you want to hear it? Might help you sell a few more books. Once we publish?'

He sighs, bracing himself for the worst, 'Go on then.'

'I put it in an email for you, as well,' she says, suspecting from the hesitant tone in his voice that this writer hated feedback, 'Overall your stories are well-written and researched with intriguing characters. My only criticism is they're too brief, they end too quickly. As the reader, I'd like to have known if Marie found love in adversity. Does she find love? Do you have a happy ending in mind for her?'

'She meets a man at the artist's market,' he begins, distracted by the fresh sheen of rain cascading down the window, 'He loves her paintings. He buys the finished picture of the snowdrops. It starts to rain. He helps her fold her easels, gather up her brushes. They dash to the nearest café. He feeds her soup. Afterwards, when the rain's stopped, he takes Marie to a cheap hotel, his bedroom. He undresses her. She poses naked for him: his sacred *Venus de Milo*. They make ferocious love on the crumpled bed. They fall in love and marry. She bears his children. She finds the love I lost...'

love

His voice trails off. He crouches on the bed, his head hung between his knees, shoulders heaving, crying unashamedly with the sheer effort of telling her the end of the story. Marie's happy ending.

Vicki recalls how she met Jewel that rainy morning in Montmartre and fell in love, the similarities with their brief affair: a bizarre coincidence, a pure coincidence: there can be no other explanation.

She wraps her arm around his shoulders, consoling him, 'That's the loveliest ending to her story. You must finish it,' she urges him, hugging him to her breasts, 'Tell me what happened to Lucy.'

He tells her, his disregard for rules spreads beyond writing to more dangerous areas. He loves the kick he gets from taking risks, gambling with his life, the lives of others: his living characters, he calls them. The hazy line between reality and fiction blurs inside his mind, making him distracted, impatient, a poor driver who takes chances driving past red lights, overtaking vehicles when the road ahead isn't clear, exceeding the speed limit. He was caught speeding by a woman community volunteer, a resident, seizing the opportunity to increase road safety awareness and reduce traffic collisions in her village, warned then forced to attend a driver's awareness course to avoid penalty points. The course should have had a lasting positive effect on his attitude, should have stopped him being reckless. He didn't heed the warnings, the danger signs. He lost control of himself, lost control of her.

Lucy agitated him. She had difficulty concentrating on the simplest of tasks. It was as if her mind was elsewhere. It made her lax, forgetful, careless, at times. He was constantly reminding her to wear her seatbelt in case they were involved in an accident. She just laughed at him, told him not to be so boring. Life's too short for cares and woes, she said.

On the day of their accident, heavily pregnant, she'd struggled with her seatbelt, given up, held it across her belly pretending to be strapped in. For once, he didn't check her. They set off for their evening baby and maternity class in Meerten. A car was parked with its hazard lights flashing in the country lane which led to the village. It was dark. The lane had no street lights. He couldn't see beyond the car. He was speeding, didn't allow himself enough time or distance to brake. He overtook the car then, too late, braked to avoid crashing into the fallen tree blocking the road. She screamed. Their car smashed into the tree trunk, catapulting her out of her seat, through the windscreen into the dark, killing her instantly. Somehow, he escaped with minor facial injuries.

Alleyn conceals them with his beard.

'I lost the woman I loved,' he says, 'Lost her baby. I'll never forgive myself for what I did to her. I fell apart, at first. I'm seeing someone now, someone loving, understanding, someone who helps me to come to terms with life without her.'

Vicki's struggling as well, struggling to come to terms with the enormity of his loss: the woman's cruel death in the dark, her dead baby. Her challenges are nothing compared to this man's torment.

'I'm glad for you,' she says, reassuringly, 'glad you're seeing somebody who can help you heal.'

He isn't sure he can trust her with the shock he is about to reveal: his sordid secret. Why not? He just opened his heart to her, didn't he? He straightens, he looks her in the eye, tells her the startling truth, 'She isn't what you think. I'm seeing a girl online. Her name's Alice. She isn't real.'

Nervously, she rubs her lips, opens her mouth, and fingers the tip of her tongue, 'Alice isn't real?'

'Alice is a flexible, adaptable, computer-generated, AI woman. I've asked her to be Lucy for me.'

For the first time in her life, Vicki is completely lost for words.

waist

'I'm sorry. I've told you too much,' he says morosely, 'I think I should go.'

'Don't! I want you to stay.'

Vicki draws his hand round her waist, draws his bearded face to hers, loving the scratch of bristled hair abrading her soft skin. She opens her mouth for him, feeling his slimy tongue sliding all over her palate, loving his sour taste, his lambent forcefulness, in her. He caresses her waist. His hands wander slowly up her torso to her breasts. She loves him touching her breasts. It makes her tingle.

They pause for breath.

He murmurs at her, 'God, it's been so long.'

She kisses him on the lips. Pecks his cheeks, his forehead. Shifting his clutching hand, she stands.

'There's no need for you to punish yourself anymore,' she says, echoing her brat's words, 'I'll help you. I *want* to help you.'

His jaw falls as she pulls her jersey over her head and takes off her bra, freeing her heavy breasts.

'Jesus Christ! You're beautiful.'

She pulls down her comfortable tracksuit bottoms squatting on the carpet between his open legs, wearing just her black hipster pants, cocks her head to one side and says, 'Well, do you want me?'

'If you're sure that's what you want?'

She eases him out of his tanned leather moccasin slippers: his feet are bare and smooth, 'It is what I want.'

He lets her take control. She rises like his sensuous phoenix, unbuttoning him, tugging his herring-bone sweater over his head. She runs the palms of her hands over his soft, matted hair, kissing his neck, chest, nipples, navel. He is well-hung, bulging, hard, jutting, out of his creased olive chinos.

She caresses him assuredly, brazenly, pulls down his trousers, pants, panting, for him, 'Love me.'

'I didn't bring my sheaths,' he says, struggling to find the right words, 'I didn't bring a condom.'

She stands, grips the waistband on her pants, and goes to pull them down, 'So? I'll take my pill.'

He gasps aloud as she pulls down her pants, revealing her sensational dark round chocolate mole. She sits in his lap facing him with her hands cradling his head, her soft breasts pressed against his chest, her pressure on him unbearable.

naivety

As soon as he has shut the door and left her, Vicki slides gingerly off the crumpled bed, a wounded snake-girl, and surveys the aftermath of her latest bout of sex. The sheets are soiled with a yukky, damp deposit from where she dismounted her eager stud, lay on her back and let him mount her in the time-honoured missionary position. She's leaking out: his seed is smeared upon her thighs. She didn't come herself: he didn't give her the time, consideration or love. Keira showed her love: her Irish brat brought her to orgasm. Disgusted by her own naivety, how she gave herself to the estranged man in her uninhibited act of wanton sex, helplessly, licentiously, promiscuously, she hobbles with her legs crossed to the toilet, pees him out of her, then takes her contraceptive after-sex pill. She showers for ages, scrubbing every last gram of his residue out of her body with an oval bar of lemon soap. Dries her hair. Wrapping a bath towel around her waist, she returns to the bedroom. She strips the bed, bundles the sheet, pillow cases and duvet cover into a soft ball, takes the ball to the kitchen, dumps it in the washing machine, adds a scoop of powder, a squirt of softener, slams the door, and sets the dial to cottons.

'Where do I go from here with him, with Keira?' she asks herself, 'How does he feel about me? Does he even care about how I feel? Care about me? Love me? Will he want me again, and again? How will I manage to stay objective about his writing after what we did? What do I say to Keira?'

She makes a supreme effort, inputting data for breakfast and lunch on a spreadsheet, calculating the food's calorific, fats, sats, carbs and protein values so that she can work out how much meal allowance she still has left for dinner. Having entered the nutritional details off the back, she takes the can of mackerel in brine to the kitchen, peels back the ring pull, and tips the oily fish onto an oval platter. Adorns the plate with freshly sliced tomatoes, pared cucumber, gem lettuce leaves, soused beetroot, olives: mustn't forget the olives which brighten up a dull salad. She is just about to drench her meal in reduced fat Caesar dressing when her phone vibrates. His text confirms exactly what is expected of her on Sunday:

Your mother and I will meet you on the westbound platform at Aigburth at 2pm on Sunday.

Try not to be late for once,

Max.

There is no love felt, no asking how she feels, no respect at all, for her: only his curt instructions. She replies succinctly with:

See you, then. Won't be late, Vic.

Putting the beast out of her mind, she screws the light blue plastic top onto the vinaigrette bottle and attacks her salad, eating slowly, taking breaks to breathe between each mouthful. She thinks of Gail pausing, a laden fork of flesh suspended in front of her mouth. On their intimate train ride, she told her the serum works by suppressing her appetite, quelling her hedonic hunger, quenching her thirst with the added benefit of reducing the risk of heart failure ensuring she feels vibrant and mentally alert, never sluggish or sleepy.

She finishes her salad, reaches for the fruit bowl and extracts four satsumas. Questions pop out of her brain like mental popcorn:

Why didn't the serum suppress her hunger?

She peels the fruit chewing it segment by segment.

Does this imply that she was cheated by Gail?

Vicki climbs off her highchair, makes herself a glass of blackcurrant squash, plucks a mango yogurt from the fridge, rips the lid then eats it, carefully, with a teaspoon.

naivety

Why didn't the treatment work? Was it a treatment at all? Was it the real thing?

Or was she sold a fake, a naïve girl's craved-for placebo?

Mind made up, she opens the cupboard and stares at the sealed phials populating the highest shelf.

Resisting the urge to smash them and taste the contents, she takes an open packet of flame raisins, and pours a handful in her palm, mixing it into her yogurt. Thinking of Keira, she checks the time. Her girl will soon be finishing her shift, exhausted after last night's sex, driving home for a good afternoon's rest. Deciding to keep her latest sexual indiscretion secret, she sends the loveliest text:

My Sweetest Girl, I wanted to write and thank you for being so kind to me. I've stopped injecting. Started using the spreadsheet. I couldn't have changed without your love. Can I see you tonight? I thought salmon and Sancerre at seven?

I love you so much, Keira,

Vicki xx

Keira replies with:

Salmon and Sancerre sounds great, Sweetheart. See you later, then. Love you lots, Keira.

In higher spirits, Vicki brews herself a milky mint tea, then retires to bed for a much-needed rest.

face

He can't get the hair right. It's either too long or too short. Too fair or too dark. The face and torso are alright. It's just her hair. Frustrated with his inability to add the finishing touches and bring Lucy back to life, he selects START OVER and creates a new face. Diligently, he moulds the moles spattering her cheeks, those lying in her hairline, the prominent dark chocolate mole on her forehead, pausing at her neck. He recalls how she led him on, letting him push his tongue inside her mouth, her honeyed taste, encouraging him to caress her naked breasts, her mole: how they made love. Next time, he'll make her *his* way with her crouched on all fours, his lioness, her sexy black hipster pants stretched taut round her knees, his hands grasping her plump waist. Hardening at the thought, he shuts his eyes, his imagination running like sweat.

She is lying naked on their marital bed, teasing him unashamedly, 'Well, do you want me?'

I don't just *want* you, Vicki. I *need* you.

If there *is* a next time.

He considers her issue: her self-created imaginary body fat, smiling in anticipation at the savoury prospect of their radical cure, checks the time in the bottom right hand corner of the screen: lunch time. Outside his closed dining room window, the sky is filling with cotton wool floating in a sea of blue. He feels the early spring sunshine warm his face. Blinks bright sunlight out of his eyes.

face

Finished with her, at least for now, he removes the memory stick bearing her finest facial features: her beguiling cocoa brown moles, then he logs off and sets off for his mystery lunch appointment.

Tears

As soon as she has finished her shift, Keira hurries to the female changing room and cries, letting her tears roll down her cheeks as far as the corners of her mouth. She finds the assistant manager, Anllela, hiding in the back office. The blinds are pulled to. The dusky Columbian beauty with trailing black hair and olive skin is sitting hunched on a chair dressed in a slinky white satin slip, hands clasped firmly round her slender calves, hugging herself. She looks up, eying her intruder suspiciously, and asks, 'What do you want? Can't you see I'm getting dressed?' softening when she sees the drying tears, 'What is it, Keira? What's the matter?'

'My dear Aunt Niamh died this morning.'

Anllela bows her head low in a simple gesture of her sympathy, 'Oh, I am sorry, were you close?'

'Very close,' Keira sniffs, 'She was a second mother to me after my mammy died. I'm afraid I've to go to Ireland for a few days for her funeral? I'm really sorry. Promise, I'll be back next week.'

A constant worrier, Anllela clasps her legs, drawing her slender calves inwards until they press against her thighs, and shakes her head, 'I can't find cover for you at such short notice.'

Keira thinks she's ripe, the sensuous Latina who paints her toenails silver, wears black rose tattoos on her wrists. Has ideas, pouts her lips, sways her hips, 'Please, Anllela, I'll make it up to you.'

Her prey raises her head, feigns surprise, and smirks, 'How will you make it up to me?'

Keira locks the door behind her, peels off her sports bra and fitness pants and tells her frustrated feminine boss how she'll make it up to her. Keira's breasts are round and pale like over-cooked dumplings. She has great abs too, pallid milk-white skin, cleft buttocks, lean sinewy thighs: a body to die for. Anllela wants her for her dollish figure, her slender athletic limbs, her sleek rakish torso. Her body unfolds like the Alien's. She climbs down off her pedestal, peels off her satin slip, and lies spreadeagled on the threadbare office rug while Keira kisses her body, all over, naughtily.

As soon as she can rediscover her tongue, Anllela immediately grants her staff her holiday request.

fetish

Gail meets Mel outside the new olive bar in the high street. They pump their brollies dry, stand them in a brass tube by the doorway, take off their waxed jackets, hang them on the back of chairs then occupy the four empty seats at their reserved table. It feels great to get out of the rain. The plate glass windows are running with molten condensation, liquifying steam. The place is full of gastronomes, all of them intrigued by the ingenuity in the menus: marinated olives, olives stuffed with crumbled blue cheese, lemon and garlic, warm olives served with anchovies, olive sourdough bread, olive juice, hot olive and chive mash, breaded blue-cheesy olive nibbles, puttanesca pasta, chicken cacciatore. Most dishes are presented on green and red plates decorated with black olives.

Olivia's Fetish is the in-place to see, to be seen in - if you want celebrity status as much as Gail.

They are greeted by the harassed-looking owner with breast-length caramel hair wearing a strappy black dress that accentuates her flat chest. Either Olivia has a serious neck injury or she was born with her deformity: she can only look left or upward, giving her a snooty, posh, snob, demeanour. She presents the menus with a twisted, know-all smile, ignoring Mel.

'Hey, you're Gail Murragh, the fatness guru, right?'

Mel corrects her, 'Fitness guru.'

'I meant fitness guru.'

Taken by surprise, Gail's shimmering gloss lips part slightly, her cheeks blush a rose beneath her freckles, and she doffs her head excitedly, 'Yes, I'm Gail. How did you know it's me?'

'I saw your topless photo on Tumblr advertising your fat loss cure, not that I need to lose any fat.'

'Definitely not, you have a slim figure. There's no fat on your boobs, belly, hips, waist and bum.'

'If you don't mind my saying, Gail, I think you have beautiful breasts.'

'She's beautiful all over,' Mel says, 'I should know. I'm the lucky girl who gets to snap her nude.'

'Shush, Mel! You're not meant to tell anyone about my modelling.'

Fascinated, Olivia lowers her voice, 'Nude? Why does she take pics of you in the nude, Gail?'

Gail hides her blushing face behind her open menu, 'I think you should take our order, don't you?'

'I think she should,' says Mel, studying Olivia's crooked posture, 'What happened to your neck?'

The entrepreneur says, accidentally still ogling Gail while addressing Mel, 'I sprained myself.'

'I can see that. How did you sprain yourself?'

Olivia shifts and spins to face Mel, 'If you must know, I sprained my neck kissing my girlfriend in bed last night.'

'Where did you kiss her for heaven's sake?'

'Where do you think I kissed her?' her face flushing, Olivia flips her ruffled order pad, sucks the gnarled tip of her biro and tells them that the special today is Lasagne Verdi served on olive bread.

She shifts to face, 'Gail?'

'I'd like olives stuffed with crumbled blue cheese, lemon and garlic to start followed by chicken.'

'Make that two,' Mel adds, 'And can I see the wine list?'

The café erupts into a shrill cacophony of young women's cries, yells, pleas and clamour for the bill, babies crying, dogs barking – Olivia's Fetish is dog and baby-friendly, has to be, and moans.

'Sorry, I have to serve the others' she says, making them sound inferior to Gail, which they are, in terms of celebrity, 'Why not finish off your Olivia's meal with a crisp refreshing glass of chilled Sauvignon Blanc with its pleasant notes of citrus and grassy herbs?'

Appreciating the girl's excellent brand awareness and marketing techniques, Mel grins at Gail.

'Suits me, Gail?'

'Just the one then. Some of us have to watch our waistlines, unlike my little dumpling.'

Mel turns red. Olivia leaves them to attend to the unruly others: a motley crue of young mother's with buggies, hound handlers, female shop workers grabbing a sandwich, a smart businesswoman.

Mel's voice falls, exploring their excuse for lunch out, the confidential conversation, 'How's our guinea pig doing?'

'She isn't responding to treatment. In fact, she isn't responding at all. Would you believe she just blocked me?'

Gail's girlfriend perks up, 'What?! After all that serum you administered and help you gave her?'

'After all my tender loving care, the one-on-one support, my personal advice on how to shed fat.'

'What do we do now? We can't just leave our baby to get any fatter. Think of all the bad publicity.'

Gail's face breaks into a cruel smile, 'Don't worry, I have a plan for her. A plan that can't fail.'

'Oh, I do love it when you have a plan. And what, exactly, do you have planned for her this time?'

Olivia arrives on cue with their olives stuffed with crumbled blue cheese, lemon and garlic and two misted glasses of chilled Sauvignon Blanc. Gail outlines every minute detail of her plan while they eat and drink. It comes as no surprise to her when her personal assistant bombards her with questions. After all, it *is* what she pays her for: to safeguard her from harm, preserve her dubious reputation, protect her from fakes, scammers, other criminals, the authorities, her angered clients.

'How can you be sure she'll be there when you expect her to be there?'

By way of an answer, she hands over her mobile, 'I had this text from Max. Here, take a peek.'

Your mother and I will meet you on the westbound platform at Aigburth at 2pm on Sunday.

Try not to be late for once,

Max.

'Max sent you this?'

'He hates her guts. Can't stand her obsession with fat any longer. He can't wait to get rid of her.'

'Okay,' Mel says, in her usual measured tone, 'Suppose she's late? What if she doesn't turn up?'

Gail gives off another cruel smile, cruel as phosgene in a confined space, 'I get a call, from him.'

They finish their starters, sip their wine, admire each other over the table. It all sounds so perfect.

'Talk of the devil,' she smirks looking over Mel's head at the opening door, 'Here he is, with her.'

Alleyn takes off his blue-gray chequered lined woollen fleece and hangs it on the back of a chair.

Just as Keira takes the last remaining seat at the table.

raw

I thought salmon and Sancerre at seven? I love you, so much, Keira. Vicki xx

Vicki wakes at six, heaves herself out of bed, pads to the sink, scrubs and sanitizes her hands. Her little heart pounding at the prospect of loving Keira again, she dresses in her black hipster pants, pulls a grubby Olio Extra Virgin Di Olivia apron on over her naked breasts and starts to cook. This is how she loves to prepare her romantic suppers: in her own good time, in the raw. She starts by mixing a ladle of honey and the juice of half a lemon into a glaze, basting the raw salmon fillets, which she has already assembled on a greased baking tray, sits them by the oven, sets the grill to high, oven to low, then lays up two trays with her mother's best silver cutlery and cut lead crystal glasses for supper in bed. A competent cook, she tops and tails some fine French beans, pares and slices some carrots, deflowers a head of broccoli, washes the baby new potatoes, and puts them all in pans to boil. As soon as the vegetables are cooked al dente, she drains them off and stores them in the oven in le Creuset dishes.

By now, she's a bag of nerves, trembling with excitement at the thought of entertaining her lover. She takes the potatoes off the boil, stores them with the sides, washes the saucepans, checks the wine has chilled to condensation misting the bottle, unscrews the cap and lets it breathe. Not that Sancerre needs to breathe.

That's Vicki for you. Full of neat little vegetal twists.

Finally, she grills the salmon fillets and sighs, 'That's dinner done, my turn next.'

raw

She pulls off her apron, washes her hands, then pads to the bedroom forgetting the curtains aren't drawn. Everyone can see her. For her romantic soiree she will dress in just a black jacket, no bra. Slipping it on, buttoning it up, tightly at the waist, she admires her fashionable self in the mirror.

'Must admit, I look amazing,' she says checking her phone: there are no new messages, the time is coming up to seven, 'She'll be here soon.'

She stands at the window wringing her hands, searching in vain for Keira in the dark. Instead, she spots a woman dressed in a waxed olive jacket standing under the lamplight, studying her bedsit, her ripe cherry red Mini parked outside, studying her. Shuddering, she quickly draws the curtains wishing someone were there to protect her. In desperation, trapped inside her own fearful mind, she calls her neighbour across the cul-de-sac, only to be told:

Hello, this is Lucy Elting. Leave your message after the beep and I'll call you back.

She can't believe it: Lucy has been dead over a year and he hasn't thought to change the voicemail. Still, she reasons, stranger things happen on Facebook where her dead friend Ruby lived on as an eternal, ethereal apparition for years making the occasional appearances for birthdays, weddings, hen nights, stags, other ghoul's memorials.

She calls Keira, only to be told:

Hey, you're through to Keira. Leave me a message. I'll get back to you.

'You're late,' she says, fussing over her, 'Where are you? Are you alright? I'm missing you.'

At nine, she reluctantly accepts, her girl isn't coming. Distraught, she takes their desiccated meal out of the oven and picks at remnants of the fish, like a starving carrion crow tearing rotting flesh off a corpse.

feast

She puts on her black bra, a soft cream tracksuit, pink anklets and gym shoes, vacates her bedsit and sprints across to the mobile fish and chip wagon stationed in the pub car park on Main Street. Careful not to splash herself wet by treading in the puddles on the pitted tarmac path. The sky is shrouded in black clouds overhead as if it's wearing a widow's cloak. The temperature falls and she senses the first spicks and specks of rain in her face. She crosses the street at the zebra crossing using the end of her bedsit key to press the button in case the plastic is coated in germs - just as the clouds burst.

The culinary charabanc, a fryer's delight on wheels, stands proud: a beacon of hearty sustenance for creatures of the night who gather, like moths to the lamplight, under its towering sodium-flash FISH AND CHIPS sign. A less obvious sub-title reads FRESHLY HAND BATTERED in golden italics, as dully gold as the colour of fish batter when fried. Beneath the banner stand its luminescent blue sentinels, guardians of the hatch, or price lists.

Her eyes alight on the Battered Cod and Chips £12 and Cheese Sauce £2 ignoring the display of waldos in vinegar, cans of Diet Coke, 7-Up and Fanta and goldfish bowls of chocolate bars on the shelf above the fried fish. The interior of the wagon is decked out with fake white wall tiles giving the false impression of a bright, clinically hygienic kitchen. She feels dirty, out of place, cold and wet, standing in a huge puddle awash with greasy wrapping papers, empty cans, used paper cups, soggy cigarette butts, as the rain teems down matting her hair, sticking her wet strands to her scalp like some fragile helmet.

If only I'd worn my waterproof rambling gear. If only…

feast

There are four of them, lowlife, loitering with intent to buy, in a disorderly huddle underneath the wagon's hatch trying to stay dry, blocking her path.

The pair nearest the counter: a spotty youth in a carp angler's hat, fawn fleece and drainpipe jeans, and a plump girl with damp curly brown hair, grubby anorak and skinny jeans, torn at the knees, are arguing over whether to have battered cod, deep-fried chicken goujons, battered sausages or plain saveloys.

A tall man with oval glasses in a thick black wool coat is talking into his phone cursing the wait. An exhausted round-faced girl with saggy jowls and black bags clinging to her eyes dressed in an off-black t-shirt and soiled cardigan, appears like the dark angel's stepsister above them and asks, 'Made your mind up yet?' Finished piss-farting around?

'Maxine?' the youth says, scowling at the girl.

'Can't decide, Mick,' the girl says shrugging her shoulders.

'Me neither.'

Come on! Vicki's drenched, soaked to the skin, 'Mind if I join you and shelter out of the rain?'

'Sorry, didn't see you,' they make a space for her and order a saveloy, chips, curry sauce and two forks.

At last!

That'll be nine pounds, then,' the server says handing them a package with a pot of brown sauce.

'Nine quid? That much? Really?'

'Yes, really,' she says in a distinctively Australasian accent, pointing at the price list, 'See that?'

'It's just, I came out without my phone and don't have any cash, do I Maxine?' he says sorrily.

Maxine digs in her pockets and draws out some loose change, 'I've a couple of quid if that helps?'

Stamping her squelchy gym shoes in frustration, Vicki delves into her red leather purse and pulls out a ten-pound note.

'Here,' she says handing it to the server, 'I'll pay for them. Take it, before we all catch our deaths.'

The dead tired Australasian woman eyes her shiftily, 'Are you sure you want to, sweetheart?'

Sweetheart. She called her sweetheart – like Keira. 'Babe!'

A prematurely balding young fish fryer wearing a navy hoodie marked FRESHLY HAND BATTERED in gold letters and batter-spattered apron swivels round to face the motley crue, 'What is it, Kate?'

'This woman wants to pay for this wuss and his Sheila's saveloy. They're skint. Shall I let her?'

'How much do they owe us?'

'Nine pounds.'

'Know what?'

'What, honey?'

'I can't be stuffed.'

He shows the scruffs a middle finger and tells them to rack off out of his sight before he brains them. They vanish into the night. Vicki steps forward out of the rain. The tall man orders fish and chips with a sachet of tartare sauce, a can of 7-Up and a Twix bar. Kate asks herself who's next? 'Now, who's next?' she says, 'Yes, sweetheart?'

'A large cod and chips with extra chips, cheese sauce and a Mars bar, please,' Vicki says, hungrily.

Someone's feeling hungry tonight, 'Sure, vinegar on the chips?'

'Yes, please – lots.'

Kate arranges a huge chunk of battered cod onto a polystyrene plate and shovels on two loads of chips, dousing the lot in vinegar. She wraps it up in white packing paper, stashes it into a carrier bag adorned with a sea blue dolphin, adds the pot of sauce and chocolate bar and hands it to Vicki, 'That'll be fifteen pounds, then,' who settles by debit card and turns to go.

'Oh, and Vicki,' Kate adds.

Vicki wonders how she knew her name? The gym, she decides, she must be using the gym, 'Yes?'

'It was kind of you to offer to pay for those bludgers just then. Take care of yourself, sweetheart.'

'I will,' she says staring into an empty abyss of loneliness, knowing she's about to go off the rails, 'I will take care of myself.'

An aged bald man in baggy trousers, open-toed boots, hauling a black bin liner over his shoulder, slumps against the wagon shelf, waving his cigarette butt at her. He shows her his soiled placard: Homeless. Please help me. Any way you can.

Strained, welling up, bursting out with spent emotions inside, Vicki can't take any more tonight. She leaves him to survive as best he can on the empty, flooded streets of Elting. When she gets home, she peels off all her wet clothes leaving the sodden pile on the kitchen floor, goes to bed and gorges on fatty fish and chips, cheese sauce and chocolate. Falls asleep: flatulent, nauseous, despondent. The asp appears on her pillow at 03:15, hissing, spitting at her. Terrified, she breaks into a cold sweat, tries to flick the beast off her before it bites. The pale pink asp curls up into a ball, the ball turns into a human head, the head grows a girl's face she knows as Keira's.

Her cheese sauce inspired nightmare over, she weighs herself as a punishment. She's put on five pounds tonight. Her phone buzzes. Surely, things can't get any worse? She has one new message: Sweetheart, so sorry for tonight. Aunt Niamh died this morning. We were close, very. She was a second mother to me after mammy died. I've had to fly back to Ireland for a few days to attend her funeral. Should be back Monday?

Be seeing you, then.

I love you, Vicki.

Promise, I do, Keira.

binge

After three more days of binge-eating The Bakery's scrambled egg and sausage brioche, Olivia's stuffed olive, tomato, pesto and mozzarella ciabatta, The Wagon's hand-battered cod and chips, a plethora of sugary drinks and chocolate bars and caramel custard doughnuts, lying around in bed, watching late night movies, Vicki slowly emerges from the constipated bowels of her depression.

Life without Keira to love has no clear purpose or direction. Other than her occasional forays to local shops and takeaways, she is a virtual recluse.

The tell-tale scales lie discarded on the shower room floor. She dreads to imagine how much fat she has packed on. She pinches several inches of flab around her waist, feels heavy in her breasts, wondering if her period is due, knowing full well it came three weeks ago. She stands in front of the bedroom mirror, crying at her fresh midriff bulge, 'Can't let them see me like this, just can't.'

Then she remembers, this afternoon she's meeting her mother with odious Max for afternoon tea: dainty smoked salmon sandwiches in triangles, sultana scones, jam and clotted cream, chocolate eclairs bursting at the seams with whipped dairy cream.

'Must get some exercise, just must.'

She dresses in her black hipster pants, a plaid cotton shirt, skinny jeans, soft anklets and trainers. At eleven, she steps out of her hovel, its bed, sink, hob, highchair and shower. Today, if she really applies herself, and concentrates, she could finish her brisk country walk in record time, come home, change into her Sunday best and catch the early train. In good time to greet her mother and beastly brother on the southbound platform at Aigburth. She edges open the door, and searches for suspicious signs of life.

'Please, tell me I'm alone. Tell me she isn't here today.'

For once, Gail isn't there. She sighs with relief, locks the door securely behind her, saunters over to her sweet little ripe red cherry car, and climbs inside.

'I *am* alone. Gail isn't here for me today, must be taking her day off. After all it is my lovely day.'

It *is* her lovely day: the sabbath, lucky for some, a mild, sunny, warm in the sun, cool in the shade day, a light breeze blowing loose stray hairs off her face. Heartened, she switches on the ignition, tunes the radio, listens to a traffic report, an eighties love song, switches it off, and drives through the quiet market town. A few resident joggers, dog walkers, café posers mainly, are up and about, chatting, eating brunch. Her mind drifts. Vicki shifts her eyes and concentrates on the road ahead. Her head aches. She rubs her tired face wishing she were safely in bed. The car swerves, catching the kerb. An old woman curses her on the pavement. The car behind flashes its headlights. A driver gives her horn. She puts her foot down, changes to third, motors off from all of them, fast, furious, wild, free.

'Nasties, all of them! Why can't they be kind to me? Why don't they understand me? Road hogs!'

Half an hour later she reaches a church. Its deserted car park borders a serene graveyard swathed in carpets of bluebells, dying daffodils. Two men dressed in bright red safety helmets fitted with tinted protective visors and orange jumpsuits that remind her of the non-compliant detainees at Guantanamo Bay are cutting back an overgrown yew tree that is obscuring the church porch.

The eldest of them wolf-whistles at her and calls to her, 'Hello, beautiful girl, fancy a stroll?'

Ignoring him, she winds up the window, climbs out of the car and slams the door, storming off in a huff. Soon she reaches the start point of the walk: a horse-proof metal gate she has to draw apart without catching germs in order to enter the field. Gates represent a challenge for her - like Gail. For one, uncertain moment, she wishes Gail were there to help her get in – then again, she doesn't.

'Is it clean? Tell me the gate's clean, I don't want to catch a lurgy. Gail's unclean. I know she is!'

Gail - who reached out to her and held her hand. Gail - who asked her if she could be her friend.

She shakes the creep out of her mind, forces her plaid shirt cuffs into the jaws of the horse-proof gate and enters the field. There are ten ponies in the field, one of them a piebald, one a Shetland pony. Vicki wonders if they are placid, easy-going, good-natured, docile: as docile as she behaved on the train for Gail who led her on. Why didn't she just shrug off her attention, use negative body language, stay her advances with her raised hands, instead of misleading the eager woman into believing she was attracted to her? Since then, she has failed to shake Gail off. The bloodhound is constantly sniffing her out as if tracing her scent, her musk. Following her everywhere from the silence of the library to the market, shops, nature reserve, cafes and bars. Gail who waits for her in the cul-de-sac for her to re-enter her world. She hasn't told a living soul about her shadow. For fear of getting hurt? Or is it a more private fear than that? A fear of losing her as a source of help?

The field is muddy in places, split in half right down the middle by a boggy ditch she has to cross. There is a grand country house with stables overlooking her, nobody about, as far as she can see, no dog walkers or lovers holding hands. Paying heed to her brand-new trainers, she ponders over what to do next.

'Now I'm going to get all muddy. How could I forget my boots? Why am I always this stupid?!'

Undetered, she pulls off her trainers, socks and jeans and wades through the knee-high, muddy water.

trust

She trusts Bryce, likes him a *lot*, but doesn't love him. He is always gentle, caring and considerate with her. Above all else, she trusts him inside her when they perform for the camera. After they've finished, she always thanks him, kisses his sweaty ebony forehead, turns, then thanks her female photographer, Mel. Gail insists on having a female behind the lens for all of her shoots.

Mel blushes and smiles and says, 'You're welcome, Gail. You were perfect, lovely as ever, great!'

Bryce is dripping with thick sweat, 'Are you sure you won't us for lunch? The game is very good.'

Gail disentangles herself from her stud and swings her slender legs off the bed. The sheet is wet, dirty, soiled. She'll have to put a wash on after they leave. Bryce is right. The game, particularly the wild venison, at the exclusive appointment only converted stables in the meadow, Her Brace, is excellent, a gastronomic opportunity, too good to be missed. Added to which, the restaurant is only open when there is an r in the month, as is the case today. She hears the antique clock in the hall strike eleven, standing suddenly, aware, she has a meeting to attend. She gracefully declines.

'Thanks Bryce, Mel. I can't this time. I'm meeting someone. Someone very close to my heart.'

Mel, a stunning redhead of apparently unstained purity, feels for her glasses in her hair, casts her brown eyes from side to side, and gasps with fake intrigue, 'Close to your heart? How romantic! I wonder who that might be?'

'Be patient Mel. You'll meet her, here, in all her glory, later. Ready and waiting for you, and me.'

Bryce pulls on his jockey shorts, studying the gorgeous woman he just made love to, he likes to think, love for money. He feels blessed, having loved a beautiful woman like her, a classy model, at the peak of her profession. If you call having sex for a camera professional. Gail has a face that breaks men's hearts. She breaks his heart if he's honest: the straggly mess of auburn ginger hair caressing her narrow shoulders, haunting grey-green eyes, her surprised looks, pursed, puckered, kissable lips, freckles, dozens of them, smattered all over her feint-tanned chest, her cute, round, pert, little breasts: her greatest natural assets - in his opinion.

For the shoot, he'd undressed her, disrobed her, teasing her body in front of the barn window. Her tanned skin had caught the warm spring sunshine as he tugged her t-shirt off over her head. He'd ripped off her skinny jeans revealing her bespoke creation: the orange rose lingerie, handmade to match her gorgeous, freckled skin, her sublime tumbling hair. Gail had let him hold her, let him press his hard ebony body against hers, let him kiss her, invasively, until she was ready to reveal her intimate charms to Mel's prying lens, tear off his Calvin Klein shorts, and climb on top of him.

Her plan is about to go live. She pads across the luxury starlight beige carpet to the bathroom door pausing, thinking to herself for a moment, ruminating on pleasures to come, their unspoken risks.

Mel screws up her face in concentration, rolls her eyes, playing with the broad beige braces that displace precisely either side of her ample breasts. She is wearing her white, short-sleeved shirt, pearl choker, thick rouge on her lips, brown baggy trousers: feminine combinations that meet with Gail's approval. Another time of day, tonight maybe, she'll invite Mel to stay, to come to her bed.

Mel persists, 'How will you catch her? How do I know you're not teasing me, as you always do?'

Why can't you just go? Why do you always interfere? Gave you all my body's secrets, didn't I?

'I'll text you all the juicy news when I get back. Must get ready,' tarnished Gail calls, sliding off to the bathroom, 'Help yourself to coffee. I bought hot cross buns and homemade marmalade at the village market for you yesterday, butter's in the larder, dumpling. Enjoy your pheasant, Bryce'

He'd pulled himself out of her at the last moment. She stands in the shower rinsing him off feeling no guilt or shame just a mild residual ache in her stomach. It's a job, an occupation that's all, her means to an extremely wealthy end. She washes her hair, considering the benefits of her rise to fame: a name on millions of men's and women's lips, fashion icon, catwalk model, artist's model, nude model, a blemished rising starlet.

A grateful patient at the local hospital had suggested Gail, an underpaid, overworked nurse, take up part-time modelling to augment her pay, and treat herself to a few luxuries. She'd approached an agency, sent them a smart portfolio of tasty photos produced by Mel and been snapped-up. The rest was history. Mel had inspired her to success, cautiously at first, starting off with fashion shots, alluring facial portraits, moving on to tasteful topless photos, full frontal nudes, the inevitable sex. In little more than three years Gail, twenty-seven-years-old, quit nursing, had earned the deposit on an isolated converted barn in the meadows, complete with duck pond, and invested in a blue metallic Mini Cooper S Countryman with tinted windows.

By the time she has taken her la tarte noir pilule contraceptif pour son après-sex, dried herself, thoroughly, flossed, inter-dented, brushed her teeth and put on her make-up, her friends have left.

rat

Vicki dries her feet in the long grass enjoying the sun on her legs, gently colouring her olive skin, skin, a skin that's susceptible to blackened moles if she isn't careful. That's her problem: she isn't careful enough. The skin specialist at the clinic warned her to take precautions against the sun, using high factor sunscreen whenever she leaves the annexe. In her rush to leave the hovel, she completely forgot to apply the cream, bring a hat, wear sunglasses to protect her failing eyesight. Her skin prickles in the heat. She dresses and makes for the metal kissing gate in the far corner of the field, a shady place obscured by hawthorn bushes where she can pause, recover. A sign next to the clump of trees on her right reads:

Private Nature Reserve. No dogs allowed. Please take care not to tread on the bluebells when they are in bloom when walking through our woods.

The flooded stream skirts the trees creating a natural border, separating the footpath-around-the-field from the nature reserve. Her heart uplifts: the woods are carpeted with swathes of bluebells.

'Gail left me flowers: red roses,' she recalls, 'In front of my gate. She left me her calling card.'

'All Because I Love You' – Gail

The flowers of romance? She smiles, just a little, frowning, shuddery, shivery, shrivelling inside.

She can't possibly love me, barely even knows me. We touched hands. No, she reached out and touched *my* hand. I did nothing to give her the impression I was interested in her. She asked me to be her friend. I didn't, couldn't speak. She took my silence for yes. I just took advantage of her.

Her mouth is parched. She didn't think to bring a drink. She can't stand the bluebells any longer: what the spray of flowers represent in her admirer's mind, her heart, for Valentine's. The bluebells lose their natural beauty, just as she lost her joy of Spring, besotted, lost without her missing lover.

There are foxholes, rabbit warrens, badgers dens, set deeply into the bank, under the hedgerows.

Must come back at night with torch and camera, take some photos of the badgers at play. Even as she thinks up the idea, she knows forays into the countryside at night, here, are out of the question. Since her re-initiation by Gail with the cheap bunch of roses, she seldom ventures out after dark.

The converted barn with its floor-to-ceiling glass windows overlooking the meadow looms up in front of her. The couple's liberal movements, their carefree, couldn't-give-a-damn-who-sees-us, mating display, openly parading themselves, tempts her in to take a closer look. There is a privet hedge yards away, a short distance from the barn.

Vicki, who only loved a man once in her life, crouches behind the hedge watching them have sex.

He undresses her, disrobes her, teasing her body freely in front of the window. Her tanned skin glows in the warm sunshine. He tugs her t-shirt over her head. He rips off her jeans revealing her gorgeous, freckled skin, her sublime tumbling hair. She holds him, pressing his ebony body closer to hers. She kisses him. She takes off her bra, revealing her perfect breasts.

Stunned, the voyeur skulks away like a rat, hiding behind the privet hedge until she is out of their view, missing all the closed circuit tv cameras hanging off the fir trees: perverse yuletide lanterns. Her obsessed fan watches as she leaves the scene and goes off in search of a friendly tree to hug.

needs

She has the potential to fulfil her lustful needs and strange desires. She matches her requirements. Not that she is perfect. She's clumsy, and clumsy girls tend to be careless about issues like privacy, discretion and personal security. So careless that she let Gail into her life, playing into her hands.

Best of all, Hart is predictable, a creature of habit who performs the same dull rituals every day: She leaves her bedsit, next to the shared student house in the quiet cul-de-sac, turns into the high street, enters the grocery store, reappears with a giant value bar of fruit and nut chocolate and grab bag of crisps, and starts to eat.

Vicki is still eating when she crosses the road at the red light, jabbing at the button with her cuff to keep her hands clean. Today, she's smartly dressed for the sunshine in her crisp fashionable black jacket: low-cut to show off her heavy breasts to her admirer. She isn't wearing her bra, Gail notes, just a string of pearls around her neck, the tiniest black shorts, polished shoes. Her face and torso have been fattened with junk food to childish puppy fat creating a youthful allure about her which she finds irresistible:

Her accumulated body fat levels tell me she's ready for me to take her home. She's in her prime!

Gail reflects smugly on how easily she downloaded Hart's personal details off her social media, scanned her bank details off her debit card, stole her identity off her driving licence, as they sat touching thighs on the train.

needs

She follows the twenty-seven-year-old, single, in-credit girl down the fifty-four stone steps into a secluded shady recess on the tarmac footpath, the last leg of her quarry's journey into bliss, runs up to her side, and says: 'Hart, you dropped your bank card.'

Heart? Someone called me heart: how lovely, how wonderful. No-one ever calls me heart. Heart!

Hastily, Vicki stuffs the chocolate and cheese and onion crisp foil wrappers into her trendy clutch handbag and turns to face Gail, who gives her a smile, and holds up an identical bank card to hers.

Her lips move silently, it's you.

'Yes, it's me, your flexible friend.'

Quickly, Gail discards the fraudulent card, throwing it on the ground, glances around: there's no-one there. Why should there be at three pm on a Sunday afternoon? Just her target girl. Confused, disorientated, alone with her friend, her eternal, persistent, unwanted travel companion. She tries to escape. Gail is too fast for her, pulling out her drug primed loaded syringe, stabbing her in the thigh, depressing the plunger, soothing the purging fluid into her flesh, her bloodstream, easing out the needle, crushing the tube with her trainers. Vicki's stunned body slumps against hers. Gail thanks the vandals for doing all her dirty work for her by tearing down the chain-link fence that separates the path from the car park.

Hauling the unconscious girl through a hole-in-the-fence as far as her inconspicuous used car: the battered black Polo, she unlocks the door to the front passenger seat, bundles the inert body inside, does the seat belt, shuts the door, climbs in, and motors off. Careful to adhere to the speed limits, she glances at the beauty slouched in the grease-stained seat beside her, imagining all their games.

'Think of all the games we can play,' she laughs, rubbing her prey's fleshy, pudgy thigh as she shifts up a gear.

strain

'Max, how lovely to see you!'

'Lovely to see you, too. How're you keeping, okay?'

'Oh so-so, you know, can't complain. And you, darling? How are you? Not too busy, I hope, with those accounts of yours. You know how I worry about you and her.'

Worrying is an understatement. Annette Charleston (she reverted to her maiden name when her husband committed suicide), doting mother, and grandmother of two, lives in a constant state of hyperactive anxiety, intense worry for her family's safety. There are so many horrid reports in the media these days: murders, rapes, abductions, of women, children, men. She wonders what the world is coming to sometimes. It wasn't like that in her day. Her mother taught her the meaning of love, care, compassion and respect. She switches her attention from her daughter for a moment, turning her attention to her son, 'Well, Max?'

'Work's really busy, Mum,' he admits, 'We're up to our eyes in tax returns at the moment.'

Truth be told, and unusually for a mother with a daughter, and she shouldn't have favourites, her son is her favourite child. Max followed in his late father's footsteps to grammar school where he excelled at maths and statistics, then trained to be an accountant in a prestigious firm in The City. At the age of twenty-seven, he met his partner Claudia, also an accountant, and fell in love with her. They set up their business in a single room overlooking the high street in a well-to-do coastal village in Essex. The girls arrived later. To all intents and purposes, Max has it all: a loving wife and mother to their lovely children, a five-bedroom house on the coast, golden retriever, a dinghy moored at the local sailing club, ski trips abroad in winter, wild swimming in the spring, summer holidays in the sun, afternoon tea in five-star hotels once a month.

The same can't be said of his sister. Vicki can best be described as vulnerable, unpredictable and liberal, a free spirit, too liberal for her own good.

Annette glances at the station clock, shielding her eyes from the glary sun. The train will be here in a minute. Her daughter will climb out and wave, they'll all climb aboard then the three of them will hug and kiss, letting the train take the strain as they make their way to London and afternoon tea on Max, always Max. It feels unbearably hot. She shies into the shade of the canopy, dabbing at her cheeks with a floral printed hankie, reassuring herself that all will work out fine in the end.

'Better to wear out than rust out,' she says, 'How's Claudia coping? How are my beautiful girls?'

'Claud's well. She gets tired, needs to rest, catch up on her sleep - when the girls let her. Still, it should be easier for her soon: Poppy starts school in September, Rosa is starting at a day nursery?'

'You know you only have to ask, darling. I'll be over in a jiffy.'

'I know,' he says, hollow voiced, pretending he doesn't have to take her back to the secure mental health unit this evening, 'Appreciated.'

Max puts his arm round his mother's shoulders giving her his artificial hug as the train glides into the platform, draws to a halt, its doors open - and no-one gets out. Annette feels sick as a pauper.

'Max!' she cries, gripping his wrist so tightly that he feels her varnished nails dig into his flesh.

'It's alright, calm down, she probably just missed the train. I'll see if I can get her on WhatsApp.'

This is her all over: always late never on time, no consideration for them, a law to her bloody self.

He fumbles with his phone: You're late. Where are you?

There's no response. There never is with her. He guessed there wouldn't be. After fifteen minutes he gives up trying. He studies the train indicator panel. The next train isn't due for another fifteen minutes. If she isn't on that one, they'll miss her treasured afternoon tea at the hotel. Then what'll he do: serve coffee and sticky brownies in the nearest caff, tea and biccies in the bloody tea room?

He squares his shoulders, 'Must have her phone turned off.'

'Do you think she's alright?' Annette keeps saying, 'Please tell me she's alright. You know how I worry about her. It isn't as if she can defend herself - not like normal people.'

'I'm sure she'll be fine, Mum,' her son assures her, sickening in the gut, retching bile, as he stays her shaking hand.

He's lying. He thinks of the text he recklessly sent when he finally lost his patience with his sister, lost his tenuous grip on his placid self-control - and shared their rendezvous details with his lover:

Your mother and I will meet you on the westbound platform at Aigburth at 2pm on Sunday.

Try not to be late for once.

Max.

Now? He isn't really sure at all.

soon, she must

She lies dormant. Inert. Incapacitated. Immobilized by the drug she was injected with when she was caught. She feels the hard, smooth, lump lodged inside her mouth, the tube inserted down her throat. She cannot speak. But she *can* still feel the needles, soft tubes worming from her flesh, the radiant warmth spread out like a thermal blanket over her face and body, the soft straps round her elbows, wrists, thighs and ankles. Her tear trough is moist. Her eyelids feel sticky, stuck, shut, as if they're glued to her undereye, impossible for her to open. At least, she isn't hungry, or thirsty. She is satiated. Her belly is bloated and distended with food. Her bladder feels as if it's fit to burst.

She exists in a constant state of uncertainty. Wondering what will happen to her next.

Soon, she must face the consequences of her self-neglect.

The dramatic events of the past hours or days weigh heavily on her mind. The brutal act of tracing, finding, intercepting her and putting her to sleep in broad daylight could only be executed with accurate inside knowledge of her whereabouts. She thinks of her brother, the callous wording of his text.

They never did get on as children. He was always his mother's favourite child, the bright spark, educated at private grammar school while she struggled to learn at state. Maxwell, who stood to gain the family inheritance when their mother passed on to a kinder, more forgiving place. There was no love lost between the siblings and he'd grown distant from her, impatient with her constant obsession with fat. He'd be glad to get shot of her. He could have met Gail, somehow, (maybe he acted as her accountant?), and shared the vital details of their family day out. That in itself didn't guarantee that she arrived at the empty stretch of footpath in time for her assailant to spring out on her like a wily cat waiting to catch a rat as she left her hole.

No, there had to be someone closer to home, an accomplice who could relay her exact movements from the time she left her little hovel in the cul-de-sac. She thinks of the young widower lurking in the house across the road, standing behind the window, weeding the lawn, dead heading his roses, trimming his hedge, watching her. The lonely author she fucked in her darkest hour of need.

The place in which she is being stored is close, stifling hot. Her flesh feels clammy, itchy, moist, oozing with perspiration. She senses someone near her. Feels a soft pudgy hand stroke her cheek, as soft as a baby's hand. It's the first time she has felt anyone touch her since her abduction. The touch calms her, revives her, lifts her spirits. She is overcome with emotion, relief that someone cares about her. Her tear trough is moist: the tears roll freely out of the corners of her eyes, down her cheeks. The hand brushes her face. She hears a sweet voice: immature, rich, plummy, babyish:

'Hello, I'm your nurse. Wipe away the tears, shall we? Please don't cry. Hurts me to see you cry. Cry, baby bunting, daddy's gone-a-hunting, gone to find a fat-free skin to wrap his little baby in.'

Her heart races at the threat contained within the nurse's rhyme. Her mind fills with terror. Dread! She feels her body tense, relax, then tense again as the immature hand grips her arm, holding her stiff, numb limb still while a needle is slid into the crease of her elbow. Her limbs and torso jellify, go limp, heavy, useless to her. She calms. She feels sleepy. She just wants to lie in bed and sleep.

She feels her arms being gently lifted and washed with a warm soapy liquid, a soft flannel rubbing her skin clean from the webbed spaces between her fingers as high as her hairy armpits. Her chest, breasts and belly are splashed with refreshingly hot liquor, lightly bathed then dried by her caring nurse. An unbridling sense of purity, a deep serenity, descends upon her. She is at peace. She feels safe. Is in comfort. Her mind smiles cheekily as the soft pudgy hands delicately loosen the coarse leather straps wrapped round her thighs and ankles and pull off her black hipster pants.

'Oh, you've messed yourself. Let's get you spick and span, shall we?'

Spick and span? Her nurse washes her front, rolls her on her side, scrubs her back, then dries her beautiful body from top to tail with a soft, fluffy-feeling, towel.

'There!' she says, 'All done! Night-night! Make sure the bugs don't bite! See you on the morrow!'

She recoils at the sordid threat: are there bugs, here, in this bed, about to crawl all over her body?

Her nurse leaves her to rest awhile. The sedative takes effect, and she falls into a dreamful sleep. She feels a hand gently caressing her breasts, massaging her waist, rubbing her belly, making her body sing with an erotic arousal, sensual thrills that flow and ebb over her skin in confused ripples: pleasure mixed with fear. The hand grasps her soft inner thigh, kneading her flesh as if she were dough, scaling her leg, intimately, until its fingers reach her cleft.

She hears him say, 'God, but you're beautiful.'

She cocks her head slightly to one side: a persistent memory penetrates her anaesthetized mind. In her dream, she is squatting on her carpet between his open legs, wearing just her black hipster pants, cocking her head to one side, asking if he wants her? She eases him out of his tanned leather moccasin slippers: his feet are bare and smooth. She needs him. He lets her take control. She rises for him, tugging his sweater off over his head, running the palms of her hands over his soft, matted hair, kissing his stubbly neck, his hairy chest, his tiny red nipples, his navel. In her dream, he is well-hung, bulging, hard, jutting out of his creased chinos. She caresses him assuredly, brazenly.

She feels his finger moving inside her, even as she lies hallucinating, in her semi-conscious state.

Her silent liaison is interrupted by a young woman's voice, 'What the fuck are you doing to her?'

'I thought she might be in need of a man.'

'Get out!'

'As you wish.'

She feels him pull his finger out of her. Feels soiled, ashamed of herself for leading him on. Same time, she feels an unburdening, an overwhelming sense of relief. Feels exhausted, if she's honest, which she is at heart: a truthful, honest girl who just wants her body to be perfect, like the skinny fashion models she follows on social media.

She wakes to feel someone pressing the tip of a blunt instrument into her fleshiest bits: her breasts, hips, tummy, thighs and buttocks. It feels as if her body is being marked or scored. Why? For fun, amusement, for someone's perverse notion of self-gratification? She feels as if the fattiest bits of her torso are being coloured in, as if her flesh were a child's colouring book, painted, or tattooed.

To her astonishment, she smells the unmistakable putrid aroma of Keira's cheesy breath soiling her nostrils, her eyelids being pecked affectionately by her waif, her lovebird. Since she is fully intubated at the moment, she can't really be kissed on the lips. Instead, she is blessed: with soft kisses on the moles lying within her hairline, on her neck, shoulders, chest and breasts. Her brat's lips brush her right ear, she attempts to explain her original promise: There's no need for you to punish yourself anymore, I'll help you. I *want* to help you, in a guilty-sounding, regretful, tone:

'I'm sorry it had to come to this, sweetheart. I do love you, promise. But I really think it's for the best? You try your hardest, know you do. But you give in to temptation too easily, you give up. I knew that when we were holding hands by candlelight. How did you manage to eat all that cheese? Did it not occur to you that millions of women and children are dying of starvation? Have a heart. Alleyn told me about the biscuits you ate. How you fucked him in the heat of the moment? I still can't understand how you could do that to me after we had such great sex. You told me you loved me. You do love me, don't you? Anyways, you won't be seeing him again. Mel's a professional photographer,' her voice lowers, 'She caught him in the act, assaulting you, on video camera. You didn't consent, did you? Couldn't really, could you? I stopped him, just in time. He's left, gone away. If he ever so much as touches you, I'll kill him, I swear I will. I know Gail. We met at the gym. That's how all us girls meet these days, isn't it? At the gym, toning-up, keeping fit, shedding fat? Kate, the girl at the fish bar, told me about your feast the other night. If I made you go off the rails, I'm sorry. I wouldn't want to hurt you for the world. But the radical surgery on your fat is for your own good. Sometimes, darling, we all have to be cruel to be kind.'

She shudders. Her whole body starts to shake. Keira talks in riddles: goodness, cruelty, kindness, radical, surgery, on her fat? What radical surgery? Before she can give the matter further thought, she feels a needle being slid into the vein in her neck, the sedative takes effect and she passes out.

Gail performs the operation to remove her unwanted body fat from the areas she found hardest to trim through exercise and diet: her buttocks, breasts, hips, thighs and stomach. She starts off by injecting the bits of body where the fat is to be removed with a liquid containing anaesthetic and medicine to reduce blood loss, bruising and swelling. She then breaks up the fat cells using a high-frequency vibrator, a weak laser pulse and a high-pressure water jet. Satisfied that all the fat cells have been broken down, she makes a small incision in the right breast, inserts a suction tube attached to a vacuum machine, and moves the tube back and forth to loosen the fat and suck it all out. Once all the fat has been sucked out, she drains off any excess fluid and blood, stitches up the breast then bandages the treated area.

It's sweltering hot in the kitchen. Gail mops her brow with a clutch of sanitized lemon wipes, takes off her surgical mask and drinks a glass of chilled mineral water. Once she has scrubbed the blood and fluid off her gloves in the wash hand basin and put on a fresh mask, she nods for Mel to pass her the vibrator. Gail sets to work with renewed vigour, breaking down all the fat cells in the left breast, sucking out the fat, blood and fluid, stitching and bandaging it before moving on to excavate, dig, suck, and extract all the fat out of the stomach, hips, waist, buttocks, and thighs.

By the end of the surgery and liposuction, she has succeeded in removing all of Vicki's ugly fat.

afterward

The water is ice-cold. Keira swims as far as the chain of brightly coloured floats that stretch across the bay, touches it, swivels her body then strikes out for the black gritty beach, swimming strongly until she reaches the shore. The beach is deserted at this time of year, save for a few beachcombers paddling in the shallows, but as the late April sun climbs high in the sky and midday approaches, its rays feel unbearably hot on her pallid skin when she clambers out of the sea's swell. Vicki is waiting for her, holding an outstretched beach towel. She is wearing a slim-fitting black swimsuit and she looks absolutely stunning. She smiles lovingly at her brat, and asks, 'How was it, Keira?'

'Freezing! You should try it, it's good for the skin.'

'I can't swim,' she admits, wrapping her girl's lean torso tightly in the towel 'I'm not much good at anything really, am I?'

'You're good enough for me, Vicki, and that's all that matters.'

'Do you really think so?'

'I know so, and you're very beautiful with it.'

Vicki has come so far since the operation. She's got herself noticed by several new authors who'd like her to help them publish their books. Even now, three months later, she finds it hard to come to terms with the sensational improvement in her physique, fitness, mental wellbeing and beauty. She likens herself to an ugly duckling, no, a sleeping beauty awakening from her sleep to discover a vibrant new world of happiness, personal fulfilment and contentment. She hit her targets, met her goals in the most dramatic way. She has forgiven Gail and Mel for how they treated her, every form of personal triumph has its price, but she will never forgive him for the way that he abused her. She can't even bring herself to think or say his name, without shivers running down her spine.

'I'll never forget what you did for me, rescuing me from that animal, Keira.'

'I know it hurt you deeply, sharing the evidence, but we were right to press charges. Hopefully, when your case gets to court, he'll be convicted and won't be a danger to vulnerable young women for a very long time.'

Vicki isn't so sure about that, 'Hopefully.'

Keira changes the subject, 'Can you rub some oil into my shoulders before I catch the sunburn?'

She tousles her ginger hair which has darkened to brown in the brine, dries her shoulders, tummy, back, arms, and legs, and says, 'Lie on your front, then.'

Her brat lies on her front on her towel loving the sensation of her girl basting her torso with oil as if she were a leg of lamb about to be roasted, drifting into sleep. Vicki smothers herself in lotion, lies on her back, shields her eyes and stares up at the sky. Since recovering from surgery, she has taken up tennis, joined a Pilates class, started going out to clubs, restaurants and concerts, made a friend for life in Eva, made a fresh start. Could her life get any better? Soon, she must find out.

Keira awakes, 'It's no good, I can't get comfortable. I'm burning. Think I'll go back to the hotel, get some rest. Will you be coming with me, sweetheart? You must be careful - with those moles.'

'Later,' Vicki grins, with an indefinable magic concealed within her promise that brings a naughty smile to her eager lover's lips, 'I'll sleep with you, later. I want to spend a bit of time on my own.'

'Sure, I'll see you back at the hotel, then. Enjoy yourself. Don't do anything I wouldn't do.'

She waits patiently until Keira has showered the shiny black grit off her legs using the communal shower projecting from the harbour pier, changed into her soft satsuma vest and shorts, rolled her wet ash grey swimsuit up in her towel, stashed it inside her ruddy lobster drawstring beach bag, climbed the short flight of stone steps up to the palm-tree lined sea wall, and left the scene of the crime - her private crime.

The gelateria is a short walk away from the beach, up the stone steps, past the line of palm trees, across the lethal crossing where the cars don't stop for pedestrians, along a narrow path that leads to Amalfi's main square with its street cafes, pizzeria, gift shops, bars, and magnificent cathedral. Starving, she showers and dresses quickly, covering her swimsuit with a soft pair of peach shorts, a t-shirt. She puts on her sunglasses, hurries to the ice cream parlour, then stands outside gazing through the window at the tantalising display of ice creams: more cream than milk, gelatos: whole milk mixed with cream, the colourful slabs of chocolate, praline, coffee, cacao, strawberry, crema.

She smiles to herself, her wickedest smile, 'I generally avoid temptation, unless I can't resist it.'

And then, she steps inside.